WATCH 'EM AND WEEP

Life Is a Soap Opera,

a Senior Moment Soap Opera

Book 1

By Carla Kulka

authorHOUSE®

AuthorHouse™
1663 Liberty Drive
Bloomington, IN 47403
www.authorhouse.com
Phone: 1 (800) 839-8640

Published by AuthorHouse 07/07/2017

ISBN: 978-1-5246-9797-6 (sc)
ISBN: 978-1-5246-9796-9 (e)

Library of Congress Control Number: 2017910108

Print information available on the last page.

Any people depicted in stock imagery provided by Thinkstock are models, and such images are being used for illustrative purposes only. Certain stock imagery © Thinkstock.

This book is printed on acid-free paper.

To my daughter, Kellie, for her love of soap operas.

CHAPTER 1

Twenty-three-year-old Cynthia Marshall had just gotten her two-year-old toddler, Maxwell, down for a nap. It was now quiet in the house, and it gave her some relaxing time for herself.

She was the daughter of Dr. William and Nancy Cleary. The doctor was head of the Cleary Medical Center. Cynthia was the youngest in the family, with one brother and two sisters.

When Cynthia graduated from high school, she was voted most likely to succeed. She had dreams of someday becoming a teacher like her mother, but all of that went down the tubes when she met Todd Marshall. Todd was so good-looking and had such charisma that she, like most other females, fell totally under his spell.

Todd was four years older than Cynthia, and by age twenty-seven, he was the top salesman for Jenson Pharmaceuticals.

Cynthia was stunning. She probably could have had her pick of any man. Todd obviously saw how beautiful she was with her long, silky, platinum-blond hair. She was smart, and one thing her classmates saw even more than her beauty was her kindness.

Their wedding was absolutely beautiful, a fairy-tale ceremony. The weather couldn't have been better. Even though Cynthia looked exquisite in her wedding gown, she somehow felt hesitant about the marriage. Perhaps it was because every woman thought Todd was gorgeous, and he loved their flirtation, or maybe it was the fact he thought his secretary, Lucinda Lowman, was the most perfect woman in the world.

If Lucinda was the most perfect woman to him, then why did he want to marry Cynthia? So at twenty-one, she put her dreams of becoming a teacher on hold to become his bride and live what she thought was going to be a fairy-tale marriage.

Within three months of being wed, Todd and Cynthia Marshall were expecting their first child. Maxwell Todd Marshall weighed seven pounds, two ounces at birth. He was such a happy, contented little baby from the time he was born. Cynthia loved him from the minute she saw him; Todd, on the other hand, was not the loving father she thought he would be.

Even before little Maxwell was born, Cynthia thought Todd seemed distant. If she hadn't gotten pregnant, she probably would have left the marriage before their first anniversary, but once pregnant, she wanted to give the marriage a chance. Cynthia hoped maybe the birth of their son would make Todd more attentive and dedicated to their marriage, but it didn't make a difference.

Cynthia was able to tolerate most things, but the constant calls between Todd and Lucinda when he was home were annoying her. If Lucinda wasn't in the picture, maybe their marriage might work. Couldn't Lucinda let him alone the little bit of time he was home so that Maxwell could be with his daddy?

Todd's brother, Michael, was so excited for Cynthia and Todd when he found out they were going to have a baby. Unlike Todd, Michael fell in love with Maxwell immediately. When he came over to visit, he wanted to feed Maxwell, hold him, play with him, and change the little baby. He was like a father to him. If only Todd could have been like that with Maxwell.

As Cynthia relaxed during her quiet time when Maxwell was napping, she watched her two favorite soap operas, *Days in the Lives of Our Families* and *One Life to Give*. It felt good to take her mind off of her problems and concentrate on the saga of the twisted families of her soaps.

Yesterday when *Days in the Lives of Our Families* left off, Candace and Steven Bradford had just separated after Candace found out Steven was sleeping with her sister, Taylor Jenkins. Cynthia couldn't even imagine her family being as twisted as the characters of *Days in the Lives of Our Families*.

When her first soap opera was over, she turned the channel of the flat-screen television to her second soap opera, *One Life to Give*. This was the halfway mark of Maxwell's nap. His nap was like clockwork, allowing her to watch two hours of her soaps.

As she watched *One Life to Give*, Dina Grayson was about to give one of her kidneys to her half sister, Dora Lane. Dora's kidneys were failing, and there wasn't anything they could do but a transplant operation to save her life. She was so far down on the transplant list that a match with a family member was the only option.

Although she was going through some difficult times, with Todd being distant, his late hours, his lack of being a good father to Maxwell, and Lucinda's constant interference, she was glad her unhappiness was not due to infidelity.

Just as always, when her last soap was over and the music played as the credits rolled, she heard her precious Maxwell saying, "Mum-mum."

Cynthia immediately went upstairs to his room and lifted him out of his crib. Holding him to her chest, Maxwell laid his little head on her shoulder, and she rubbed his back. She couldn't understand how Todd didn't realize how much he was missing by not sharing in raising their son.

At that time every day, Cynthia wondered if Todd was going to be home for supper on time or if he would be calling with another one of his excuses about how he and Lucinda had to work late.

She felt bad about being suspicious of him when it came to Lucinda. She didn't have any proof that he was not telling her the truth. He had worked hard to be a top salesman in his company, and she needed to trust him.

She had decided to make a nice roast, potatoes, and carrots for supper. It was one of his favorite meals. Earlier, she had mentioned what she was making for supper, hoping he would make it home to eat his favorite meal, if not for any other reason.

It was no surprise to Cynthia when the phone rang and Todd was calling to tell her Lucinda was picking supper up for the two of them so they could work on a big sales pitch. Cynthia's eyes filled with tears.

"Todd, I've made this supper just for you."

"I told you I have a lot of work to do tonight with this big account. It can mean a whole lot of cash for my pockets. You wouldn't have the great life I provide for you if it wasn't for my hard work. Sorry you went to all the bother of dinner, but I have more important things going on than making sure I am home for supper."

Cynthia heard the phone disconnect. What happened to the magnificent life Todd was going to give her? What happened to her fairy-tale marriage?

As she sat on the couch with little Maxwell in her arms, it was all she could do not to weep.

When the doorbell suddenly rang, it took her mind off of wanting to wallow in her sadness. Cynthia wiped her tears and carried Maxwell with her to answer the door.

For a brief second, she hoped it was Todd—that he had decided to come home for supper. It wasn't Todd but his brother, Michael, smiling at her and Maxwell. His smile was all it took for Cynthia to let loose her held-back emotions.

CHAPTER 2

MICHAEL SAW THE TEARS IN Cynthia's eyes overflowing onto her pink cheeks. He didn't have to ask what was wrong because he knew it had something to do with Todd. He couldn't understand why his brother was not more attentive to Cynthia and Maxwell. He considered Cynthia the type of woman any man would be happy to have as a wife and mother of their children.

Michael Thomas Marshall, an architect, reached for Cynthia to comfort her, and she sobbed into his chest. He patted Cynthia gently on the back, and sweet little Maxwell mimicked his uncle. Michael kissed her on the forehead, and Maxwell kissed his mommy on her cheek, saying, "No cry, Mum-mum."

It broke Michael's heart to see Cynthia crying over Todd. She deserved better, and little Maxwell needed to have his daddy around.

"Todd called, and he isn't coming home for supper after I made him a special dinner. I guess by now I should get used to him not coming home after preparing a big meal for him. Here I am with all this food. Would you want to stay for supper?"

"Are you kidding? I would be crazy not to accept the offer of a home-cooked meal. I gladly accept."

As the three of them sat eating dinner together, Cynthia thought about how nice it would be to have Todd enjoy sitting with Maxwell and her like this. When Todd rarely made it home for supper, it was always after Maxwell was in bed.

As she chatted with Michael, Cynthia couldn't help but wonder what it would have been like to have married Michael instead of Todd. She thought he would be a terrific husband and father. She felt guilty even thinking about Michael in that way.

Michael talked about his day at work and all about the design he was working on as an architect. He used Maxwell's blocks to show his designs and let Maxwell knock them down afterward. Maxwell laughed, and they couldn't help but laugh because he was so cute.

When it was Maxwell's bedtime, Michael helped Cynthia get him ready for bed and then read him a bedtime story. He enjoyed every minute with his uncle Michael reading to him because his uncle changed his voice with the different characters in the story.

Cynthia enjoyed listening to him too. She watched the expressions on Maxwell's face as he listened to Michael. Once the story was over, Michael kissed Maxwell good night and said, "It's time to go to sleep now. I love you!"

She didn't expect to hear what came out of Maxwell's sweet lips, "Wuv Dada!"

Michael looked over at Cynthia and saw tears once again surfacing in her beautiful eyes. He was done with his brother's treatment of Cynthia and Maxwell. She had shed too many tears over him. Michael was going to finally have it out with his brother.

CHAPTER 3

ALL THE WAY OVER TO Jenson's Pharmaceuticals, Michael thought about what he was going to say to Todd when he confronted him. As they were growing up, they had many confrontations, but none of them were ever over a woman. He had tried his hardest not to interfere with Todd and Cynthia's marriage, but he couldn't be quiet any longer, as he could see the pain it was causing his sister-in-law.

He knew Todd would be livid with him for discussing how he treated his wife and child, but he didn't care anymore. Someone had to tell him how he was hurting them, because he was oblivious to how they were constantly being ignored.

When he arrived at Jenson's Pharmaceuticals, Todd's Cadillac was nowhere in sight. Nor was Lucinda Lowman's car. Todd told Cynthia he had to work on a big sales pitch, so where were they? Maybe Todd should work on a better excuse next time he told Cynthia he was going to be working late.

Michael had his suspicions about where the two of them might be if they weren't at work. He decided to check out his theory by driving to the edge of town where Lucinda lived. Sure enough, there in front of Lucinda's house he saw not only Lucinda's car but Todd's Cadillac.

He was praying he was wrong for what else he was thinking. If what he was suspecting were true, he would be angry with his brother.

Michael hammered on the front door, and Lucinda came to the door in her robe. Lucinda looked taken back to see it was Michael. Michael didn't say a word to Lucinda. Before she had the opportunity to ask why he was there, he brushed past her through the living room to the bedroom to hunt down his brother.

Just as he expected, there was Todd in his jockey shorts, surprised he was caught with his pants down and his little rendezvous with Lucinda was revealed. Todd was about to give Michael some lame excuse, but before he had a chance to speak, Michael approached Todd and slugged him in the nose.

Michael could hear Todd's nose break and saw blood spattering on the bed sheets as Todd screeched in agony. Lucinda watched what had just taken place and started to cry as Michael came toward her. She was afraid he was going to punch her, too. She was relieved to see him just walk past her and out the door.

Michael couldn't wait to hear how Todd would explain his broken nose to Cynthia.

CHAPTER 4

M ICHAEL NEVER SAID A WORD to Todd before or after he punched him; he didn't have to because Todd knew why his brother did it.

He knew Michael wouldn't say a word to Cynthia about his indiscretions. He quickly got dressed and went to the emergency room to have his nose reset before going home.

All the way home, Todd kept trying to think of a good story to tell Cynthia about how he got the broken nose. It not only had to be good; it had to be believable.

Todd quietly walked into the house. He hoped Cynthia had called it an early evening and he would have more time to concoct his story. Unfortunately, there Cynthia sat in the living room, waiting for him.

The minute Cynthia saw the tape on his nose, she rushed over to hug him.

"Todd, honey, what happened to you?"

"I feel like such an idiot! Someone tried to take the car when I was on the way out of work. He punched me in the nose to get the car keys, but I hit him back and knocked him out. I was afraid he would get up, so I just took off rather than calling the cops."

Todd was feeling on top of the world because Cynthia seemed to be falling for his explanation of his broken nose. Unfortunately, it was only seconds before he saw the expression on her face change. His fragile little wife wasn't as gullible as he thought.

"If you got hit as you said, why isn't there blood all over your shirt? There isn't even any bruising on your hand."

It was unbelievable to her that Todd could knock someone out with a punch, let alone hit them.

He knew at that moment this was not going well. The next thing he knew, Cynthia sucker punched him right in his reset broken nose, knocking him into the end table.

Cynthia didn't say a word. She just went upstairs to bed. Todd heard the lock on the bedroom door and knew she had finally had enough from him.

CHAPTER 5

CYNTHIA HAD A RESTLESS NIGHT's sleep. She knew Todd was lying to her about what happened to his nose. Whatever happened, she felt he probably deserved it.

Todd had changed so much since they first met, and she had no idea why. He used to want to spend every minute with her, and now he seemed to not want to be around her at all. This hurt her, but him not wanting to spend time with Maxwell was more than she could take.

It was 7:00 a.m. when Cynthia woke up and heard Maxwell happily playing in his crib. She was so thankful she had such a sweet little boy even though his daddy was a complete bonehead.

The minute Maxwell saw his mommy, he stood up in his crib and smiled. Cynthia dressed Maxwell, and the two of them went downstairs to have breakfast. She was hoping Todd would be fast asleep on the couch. One thing she didn't need was a confrontation with Todd in front of Maxwell.

As she walked to the kitchen, she looked over at the couch. Todd was not on the couch or anywhere downstairs. She wondered if he had left early for work or if had even spent the night on the couch.

Cynthia felt bad about sucker punching him in the nose. She truly loved him, and more than anything, she didn't want anything to break up their family. It wouldn't be fair to Maxwell.

When Maxwell finished eating, she took him upstairs to play with his toys while she got her makeup on. They were going over to her sister's house so Maxwell could play with the twins.

Annie, Cynthia's sister, was married to Charlie, who was an accountant. He was such a great father to their twins, Annabelle and Andy. Charlie worked out of their home so he could do his job around the twins' needs. Cynthia couldn't imagine how Todd would be with three-year-old twins.

After she finished with her makeup, Cynthia and Maxwell were on their way out the door for their playdate.

Cynthia was anxious to talk to Annie about what had happened last night with Todd. As usual, Maxwell was so excited to be going to play with his cousins, whom he called Abelle and Addy.

Cynthia walked around the driver's side of the car to put Maxwell in his car seat. Her excited expression changed to shock when she realized someone had slashed the front tire.

She was just about ready to dial the police about the tire but decided to call Todd first to ask him if he wanted her to call the police. He had to be at work by now, so she called him on his office phone.

Cynthia was surprised when Todd answered instead of Lucinda.

"Todd, Maxwell and I were getting in the car to go over to Annie's for a playdate, and someone slashed the tire on my car. Should I call the police?"

She heard Todd laugh. She was stunned he would be laughing about someone slashing the tire. Cynthia was not prepared for what her loving husband said to her next.

"That really sucks, Cynthia, that your visit with your sister was spoiled."

"I don't understand why you're laughing about the tire."

"Probably because you don't see the funny part, but maybe next time you will think twice before hitting me in the nose!"

CHAPTER 6

CYNTHIA DIDN'T EVEN HAVE A chance to say anything to Todd because he immediately hung up on her after admitting he was the one who had slashed the tire.

She was about ready to burst out crying but held back from doing so in front of Maxwell. Todd might have wanted to get back at her for hitting him in his nose, but how could he disappoint Maxwell, preventing him from having the playdate with his cousins?

Was Todd angry because she doubted him? She felt bad she had reacted like she did when he might have been able to explain why there wasn't any blood on his shirt. He often had an extra shirt in his car, and maybe he had changed his shirt. Why did she always have to doubt Todd? Now, because of the way she handled things, Maxwell wouldn't be going to have his playdate with his cousins.

Cynthia tried to calm down a little before calling Annie.

"Annie, I'm sorry, but Maxwell and I can't come over for his playdate. My car tire needs to be fixed. I'll call and explain later."

"Sure! Call me later, and we'll make plans for another playdate."

Cynthia was worried Annie might want to know why the tire needed fixed. She didn't want to admit to Annie what was really happening in Todd and her marriage.

Cynthia played all morning with Maxwell so he wouldn't ask about going to play with Annabelle and Andy. She fed him his lunch and put him down for his nap. By then, she was glad to have a couple hours to think about what had transpired between Todd and her. She wanted more than anything to be able to fix things between them.

She watched her soap, *Days in the Lives of Our Families.* The story had left off with Candace's husband, Steven, in bed with her sister, Taylor:

"It feels wonderful to be with you, Taylor, and not have to make up excuses to Candace anymore."

"Candace will never let you go. She loves you too much."

"Well, she has to. I don't love her anymore. I love you, Taylor, and want to be with you. I know it hurts her, but that's the way it is."

"She hates me now, but I don't care as long as we're together."

Cynthia knew it was just a story, but she couldn't imagine any husband or wife sleeping with their spouse's sibling. Cynthia knew her sisters would never do that to her.

When she married Todd, she thought they would be together forever and nothing would ever tear them apart. She thought Todd felt the same way about their marriage.

Once Maxwell was born, Cynthia was even more committed to their marriage. She was so happy she had given him a son. One look at Maxwell, and she fell in love with him. Apparently, Todd didn't feel the same way. She couldn't help but wonder if Todd felt neglected because of the baby.

She was going to do her best to be a better wife to Todd. Maybe if she did, he might return to the man she had fallen in love with.

As she continued watching here first soap, Candace was begging Taylor to break off her affair with Steven:

"Taylor, you have always been jealous of me. When we were growing up, you always wanted everything I had. Well, you're not going to get what you want this time. This is my marriage, and Steven is my husband. We're not talking about a piece of jewelry, a dress, or even a pair of shoes. This is my marriage, Taylor, and Steven is mine."

"Candace, get a grip! He hasn't loved you for a long time. We are good together, and you need to stop thinking things are going to change. You can't make someone love you if they don't."

"How can you do this to me, Taylor? I'm begging you to break it off with him and give me a chance to save my marriage."

"I will never do that, Candace. I love him too much, and he loves me. You will never get what you want!"

Cynthia thought about how screwed up these characters were in her soaps and thought to herself once again how all that was happening between Todd and her would never be because of another woman. Never!

CHAPTER 7

At the end of *Days in the Lives of Our Families,* Candace had the final word.

"I will never give up Steven, especially to you, Taylor. I hate you for what you have done to my marriage. You will never be happy because I will make your life miserable. Steven thinks you're all it, but when I get through with you, no one will want you, not even Steven."

Now it was time for *One Life to Give* with Dora and Dina. Dina was about to find out whether or not she was an acceptable kidney donor.

"They need to hurry up with the test results on whether or not I'm a match for Dora. All this waiting is driving me crazy. They don't have time to waste."

"You need to be patient, Dina. They're working as fast as they can. Once they give us the results, you'll have to think about what you're about to do. There is a big risk for you to do this. Something could go wrong during the surgery. You might even die, Dina!"

"I understand the risk, Daddy. She is my half sister. I am not afraid for me but afraid for her. If I don't give her this chance, she will die. I don't want her to die when I can maybe save her life. Oh my, here comes the doctor. Please let me be a match!"

Just like clockwork, a perfect two hours passed quickly, and she could hear her little blue-eyed boy calling, "Mum." She went upstairs to get him up from his nap.

On her way downstairs with Maxwell, the phone rang. She thought maybe it was Todd calling to apologize for slashing her tire. If he was coming home for supper, maybe they could talk.

Cynthia grabbed the phone, but it wasn't Todd.

"Hi, Cynthia! I'm calling to see how you're doing and to thank you once again for having me stay for supper. It was delicious. I enjoyed having someone to eat with for a change, and next time Todd can't make it home for supper, just call me. I'd be happy to be his fill-in. By the way, how did Todd's meeting go last night?"

"I never got a chance to even talk to him about work. I'm sorry to say I kind of overreacted last night with him."

"What do you mean?" Michael asked. He was wondering how Todd explained his broken nose to her.

"He came home with a broken nose. He said someone tried to steal his car and hit him in the nose, breaking it. I didn't see any blood on his shirt, so I told him I didn't believe him. I guess I should have given him a chance to further explain."

Michael knew Todd would concoct some story instead of coming clean with Cynthia on how the broken nose happened. Cynthia couldn't see Todd for the liar he was—and the cheat.

Cynthia was an unbelievable wife and mother. He didn't have the heart to tell her Todd was a no-good adulterer who didn't deserve her.

"Keep your chin up, Cynthia. It does seem like a pretty unbelievable story. I'll talk to you later."

Cynthia always thought she could find a way to fix any problem, but this was one thing she couldn't fix. If she found out about the affair, she would be terribly hurt Todd cheated on her. There would be nothing anyone could do to make it go away. If there was a chance to save their marriage, Todd would have to be the one to try to fix things. He would have to be faithful to Cynthia. Was that even possible?

CHAPTER 8

Cynthia wanted desperately to have some time alone with Todd to talk about things. She wanted to apologize for not trusting him and hitting him in his nose. Cynthia hoped Todd would forgive her and she hadn't made things worse between them to where they couldn't patch up their relationship. After Maxwell had his supper and she put him to bed, she waited patiently for Todd to come home.

She sat at the table staring at her empty plate. Todd had not called to say he was working late, so she wondered why he wasn't home yet. Could someone have attacked him again? She would never forgive herself if her marriage ended with the two of them having a fight. She kept saying over and over as she waited for Todd, "Please let him be okay!"

Cynthia started crying. She needed to know he was all right. If anyone should know where Todd might be, Lucinda should. Cynthia dialed Lucinda's number to ask for her help to find him.

The phone rang six times before Lucinda picked it up.

"Lucinda, I'm sorry to call you so late, but do you know where Todd might be?"

"Where do you think I might be this time of night?"

At first Cynthia thought she had dialed the wrong number. Then it was apparent she had dialed correctly. How stupid she felt. She was speechless when she realized it was Todd's voice. Here she was in tears worrying about him, and he was at Lucinda's.

"Todd?"

"Did you think I wouldn't be able to find a place to stay? Lucinda is happy to have me stay with her. You've changed since you had the kid. I get more quality hours with Lucinda!"

Cynthia was devastated. For the first time since she married Todd, she came to the realization her marriage wasn't going to last. Her fairy-tale marriage was collapsing.

She was not so upset for herself but for Maxwell. He deserved a happy family. Todd had not been much of a father to Maxwell, and she doubted if he was ever going to change. Her life was turning into a real soap opera right before her eyes and all because of her no-good husband.

CHAPTER 9

THAT NIGHT, CYNTHIA CRIED HERSELF to sleep. Todd never came home the night before, but why would he? She had hoped he would come home so they could quietly discuss what happened between them. Even with Todd's indiscretion, she still loved him, and she hoped he still loved her enough to give their marriage another chance.

Cynthia's heart was breaking, but she smiled at her little one while she dressed and fed him. They were getting ready to go to his cousins for a playdate. She wanted to do everything in her power to keep Maxwell a happy little boy.

Maxwell was excited to know he was going to play with Annabelle and Andy. She was not looking forward to telling anyone about the problems with her marriage, but she needed to unload on someone. Hopefully, while the children played she would be able to talk to Annie.

The minute they walked into the house for the playdate, Maxwell ran to the family room to find the twins as he yelled, "Abelle … Addy!" Cynthia went in after Maxwell, and when she found him, there he was hugging the twins. Charlie was sitting on the floor playing with them.

Cynthia was glad Charlie was home so she could have a private conversation with Annie. Annie was sitting in the kitchen enjoying a cup of coffee.

The minute she saw Cynthia walk toward her, she could see something was terribly wrong.

"What's the matter, Cynthia? You look like you're upset about something."

"It's awful, Annie, and there's no one that can fix things."

"What is? Tell me and maybe I can help."

"Remember the other day when we were supposed to come over for a playdate?"

"Sure, I remember. You said you needed to get your tire fixed. Are you saying your tire couldn't be fixed?"

"I wish it was as simple as fixing a tire. Yes, I did get the tire fixed, but that isn't what can't be fixed."

"So what needs to be fixed? I'll see if Charlie can fix it."

"My tire was slashed."

"Who in the heck would slash your tire?"

"It was Todd."

"You've lost me, Cynthia. I don't understand why Todd would want to slash your tire. Was he mad you were coming over to see us?"

"No. The night before we were coming over for the playdate, he came home with a broken nose. He told me some story about someone trying to steal his car—how they had hit him in the nose to get his car keys. He told me he slugged the person, knocking them down."

"Didn't you believe Todd's story of how it happened?"

"There wasn't any blood on his shirt. I guess I should have given him a chance to explain. He does have clean clothes in his car, and maybe he changed his shirt at the hospital."

"That could be what happened, but he had no reason to slash your tire. That's just crazy. Charlie would never have done that to me or spoiled the twins' playdate. I am so sorry Todd is acting like such an idiot to you."

"I thought maybe Todd and I could talk when he came home last night. I kept waiting for him to come home, well after Maxwell went to bed. I began to worry someone attacked him again. I decided to call Lucinda to see if she knew where he might have gone."

"Did she know?"

"Lucinda didn't answer the phone. It was Todd. He was spending the night at her house while I was crying my eyes out, wondering if he had been hurt or killed by someone."

"How could he do this to you?"

"I don't know what I've done wrong."

"Honey, you haven't done anything wrong or even anything to warrant him slashing your tire. That husband of yours is acting crazy."

Annie couldn't help but wonder—if Todd was crazy enough to slash Cynthia's tire, would he be crazy enough to hurt Cynthia or even

Maxwell? One thing Annie knew for sure: Charlie would never stay at another woman's house. He would know better!

Todd had always been flirtatious toward Annie when he was going with Cynthia, and that bothered her a lot. He seemed to be too much of a playboy, and she wondered why her sister couldn't see that in him.

Cynthia was so happy and in love with Todd at the time. Annie didn't want to give her any doubts about marrying him. Now she wished she had!

CHAPTER 10

Maxwell, Annabelle, and Andy were having a great time playing with each other. They all had lunch together before Cynthia and Maxwell had to leave for home. Maxwell was so exhausted he fell asleep within a couple streets from Annie's.

Cynthia was glad she had talked with Annie even though it was embarrassing to admit their marriage was having problems.

Traffic was unusually heavy for a Monday. It started to really pour, and it was getting very hard to see. Cynthia was not far from home when suddenly a car hydroplaned, hitting them in the driver's side of the car.

Maxwell was crying in his car seat when the police and ambulance arrived on the scene. Cynthia was unconscious from the impact. The attending officer was Ben Marshall, the youngest brother of Todd and Michael.

Ben tried frantically to get ahold of Todd. When he couldn't reach him, he called Michael to see if he knew how to get in touch with him.

"Michael, this is Ben! There's been an accident."

"Are Mom and Dad all right?"

"Maxwell is okay, but Cynthia is being taken by ambulance to the hospital. She's unconscious. Todd isn't at work and isn't answering his cell phone. Do you have any idea where he might be?"

"Where are you now, Ben?"

"I've got Maxwell with me, and we're on the way to the hospital."

"I'll meet you there, Ben. I should be there in about five minutes."

When Michael arrived at the hospital, Ben was holding a sobbing Maxwell. The minute little Maxwell saw his uncle Michael, he stopped crying and smiled.

"Hi, Maxwell. Uncle Michael will take care of you until Mommy is better. Stay here with Uncle Ben while I go tell Mommy."

"Mum-mum nap," Maxwell said.

Uncle Michael responded, "Then I will just whisper in her ear."

When Michael walked into the hospital room, a nurse was taking Cynthia's vital signs. She was in stable condition but still unconscious. There were multiple bruises on her shoulder and a nasty bruise plus stitches on her temple.

The nurse left the room, and Michael picked up Cynthia's fragile hand and held it as she lay unconscious. He stood there looking at her. He thought she was so beautiful even with bruises and stitches.

"Cynthia, if you can hear me, I am going to take good care of Maxwell until you're better. You don't need to worry about him. Just get better to come home to us!" Michael leaned forward and kissed her cheek.

Michael couldn't imagine where Todd could be and why he wasn't answering his cell phone. Maybe he was preoccupied with Lucinda and didn't want to interrupt his fun.

Here was Cynthia unconscious, and Todd wasn't there for her or their son.

Cynthia and Maxwell could both count on Michael to take care of them, no matter what.

CHAPTER 11

As Michael left the bedside of Cynthia, he put his hand on her cheek and whispered, "I love you!"

He left her room and went out to the lobby to see if Ben had been able to locate Todd. Maxwell was sitting at the desk coloring.

"Ben, you might want to stop at Lucinda's house to see if Todd is there."

Michael could see the surprised look on Ben's face. He hadn't told anyone about his confrontation with Todd at Lucinda's. At this point, he didn't care who knew about Todd's cheating. All he was concerned with was Cynthia.

"I'm taking Maxwell home, and if you get in touch with Todd, tell him I've got Maxwell."

Ben put Maxwell's car seat in Michael's car. The second Maxwell saw they were leaving and Cynthia wasn't in the car, he started to cry.

"Maxwell, Mommy is tired and wants to sleep a little longer while we go play at your house," said Michael to his nephew.

Maxwell just said, "Okay."

When Michael and Maxwell arrived home, Maxwell brought out his cars for them to play with. He enjoyed playing with his uncle because he made all kinds of car sounds as they were playing. Maxwell even tried to mimic the sounds.

"I'll bet you're getting hungry, Maxwell. You play with your cars while I fix you some macaroni and cheese. We can have some applesauce with it."

Maxwell must have enjoyed his supper because he kept saying "yum" as he ate it. Shortly after they played more cars, Maxwell was rubbing his eyes.

"Are you getting sleepy, Maxwell? Let's get you ready for bed, little buddy."

Michael carried Maxwell upstairs to get his pajamas on. Maxwell handed Michael a book to read to him, but it wasn't long before Maxwell fell fast asleep in his lap.

As Michael sat there holding Maxwell in his arms, he thought about how much he loved his precious little nephew. If he could love this child so much, why couldn't Todd love him? Why didn't Todd realize how precious his child was and want to share these moments with him?

He hated even thinking that he wished Cynthia was his wife and Maxwell was his son. If they were, he would be the happiest man on earth.

CHAPTER 12

MICHAEL HADN'T HEARD ANYTHING FROM Ben about finding Todd. He was more concerned about Cynthia and if she had woken up. She needed to be okay for Maxwell.

As Michael came down the stairs, the phone rang. It was the hospital. He was nervous about answering. He was terrified Cynthia was worse.

The thought of this made him sick. He couldn't lose her, nor could Maxwell.

"This is the Marshall residence," Michael answered.

"I'm sorry to bother you so late, sir, but I'm Mary, a nurse. Cynthia Marshall has just woken up and is asking about her son, Maxwell. She is worried he was hurt in the accident."

"May I please talk to Cynthia? I'm her brother-in-law, and I am taking care of Maxwell," Michael said.

"Michael, is Maxwell all right? Did he get hurt in the accident?"

When Michael heard Cynthia crying, he wished he was there to put his arms around her.

"Cynthia, please don't cry! Maxwell is fine. He didn't have a scratch on him. In fact, he had a delicious supper of macaroni and cheese, with applesauce. Now he's fast asleep in his bed. He couldn't even stay awake for all of the story."

"Thank you so much for taking such good care of him for me. I was so afraid he had gotten hurt. Is Todd there, too?"

"No, Ben is trying to find him, but Todd isn't answering his phone."

"Todd must be pretty mad at me."

Michael wanted to tell Cynthia he sent Ben to Lucinda's house to see if Todd was there, but he didn't want to upset her.

"Cynthia, you need to get some rest and not worry about Todd right now. I promise you I will take good care of Maxwell for you."

"I know you will, Michael. I'm just upset with myself for making Todd mad. It's all my fault. Todd told me his nose was broken when someone tried to steal his car. I didn't believe him. I overreacted when I didn't see any blood on his shirt and hit him in the nose. Now, he doesn't even care that I'm in the hospital, and I've ruined my marriage."

"Cynthia, please don't cry. None of this is your fault. You were right about Todd. He was lying to you about how he got his nose broken. I found him at Lucinda's house in her bedroom. He didn't have his shirt on at the time or his pants, I might add. That's why he had no blood on his shirt. I was so angry with him I hit him in the nose. I'm sorry you had to hear this from me, but I don't want you thinking any of this is your fault."

Cynthia didn't say anything for a few minutes.

"That can't be true, Michael. I remember him at the hospital holding my hand and telling me he loved me."

"I'm telling you the truth, Cynthia. I don't want to hurt you, but Todd is a liar, and you deserve better. Todd wasn't at the hospital. I came to the hospital the minute Ben told me. I sat at your bedside holding your hand."

"Did you tell me you loved me?"

"Yes, I did. I have always loved you."

CHAPTER 13

MICHAEL WAS SO ANGRY WITH Todd for hurting Cynthia. Maybe he shouldn't have told her how he felt about her. He wanted her to know that his brother was not the man she thought he was and none of this was her fault.

She had held on to the hope that Todd still loved her, like he had before they were married. She had felt something was wrong way before Maxwell was born but didn't want to admit it. She deserved better, and so did Maxwell. If Todd was at least a good father to Maxwell, she could have put up with anything, but not to be there for his own son was unforgiveable.

There was little hope her marriage would survive. Lucinda and Todd could have each other. Michael was always the one there for Maxwell and her. How could she even have thought Todd would be saying, "I love you"? She hadn't heard him utter those words since they first got married.

"The hospital will probably be releasing me tomorrow. Can you take care of Maxwell until then, or do you want me to call one of my sisters?"

"I have everything under control, Cynthia. I enjoy taking care of Maxwell. Call me in the morning when the doctor is releasing you, and we will come pick you up."

"Thanks, Michael. I appreciate you being there for me."

"I will always be there for you."

Cynthia didn't get the fairy-tale marriage she had once dreamed of with Todd, but she wasn't going to give up hope that someday she would be with someone who loved her and Maxwell.

CHAPTER 14

WHEN BEN ARRIVED AT LUCINDA'S, Todd's car was nowhere in sight, and no one was home. He stopped by Jenson's Pharmaceuticals to see if Todd was at work. They told him Todd and Lucinda Lowman called off. Ben wondered if they were a couple, as Michael had said. He never thought Todd would have an affair.

Benjamin Alexander Marshall was the youngest of the three brothers. He was twenty-six years old and had been a cop for three years. There had always been a lot of competition between Todd and Ben. They had gotten into a lot of fights, especially over girls.

Cynthia and Ben met at a concert. They were dating for just a short time when they went on a double date with Todd and his girlfriend, Linda Morris. Todd thought Cynthia was stunning, and it didn't take long for Todd to make his move on her.

Before Ben knew it, Cynthia and Todd were madly in love and walking down the aisle. Ben had a few girlfriends since Cynthia but maintained his focus on being a cop.

Even though things didn't work out between the two of them, Ben was happy for Todd and Cynthia. He just couldn't fathom why Todd would ever cheat on Cynthia. Could there be a chance Michael was wrong about Todd being with Lucinda?

Ben called Michael to let him know Todd and Lucinda were not at work. Michael was not the least bit surprised after the week's prior events with Todd and Lucinda. Michael told Ben the good news about Cynthia being awake and possibly being released in the morning.

Ben knew Michael cared deeply for Cynthia and Maxwell, because of the way he was always talking about them. As long as Todd was in the picture, he knew Michael would not interfere in their marriage.

If Todd was fooling around on Cynthia, Ben knew their parents would be extremely upset with Todd for cheating on her. Both Ken and Lorraine loved Cynthia like she was their own daughter.

Ken and Lorraine were on vacation in Hawaii for another two weeks. Ben could only imagine how his parents would react when they found out what Todd had done. Their mother would probably start crying, and their father would be reading him the riot act about breaking apart the family foundation. The two of them would probably even try to convince Todd to try to make his marriage work, even though they knew it was hard to make Todd do anything he didn't want to do. In the end, their parents would forgive him as usual, but it would take time.

In the midst of all this mess, the real concern would be about Maxwell's happiness and well-being. They would not want their grandson to have to pay the price for his parents' breakup.

CHAPTER 15

THE NEXT MORNING, MICHAEL WOKE up hearing Maxwell playing in his crib. It just made Michael smile because it was a wonderful way to wake up, hearing his nephew's sweet voice.

Someday he wanted to be the father in a house full of children. Of course, he would have to have a wife who wanted lots of children, too.

The thought of having a wife excited Michael because he was ready to be married. When he did marry, it would be forever, and they would have many beautiful, precious children, as special as Maxwell.

As Michael walked into Maxwell's bedroom, he saw a big smile on Maxwell's little face the minute he saw his uncle. This lit up his heart.

Michael lifted Maxwell up in his arms and gave him a big hug.

"Good morning, Maxwell. Uncle Michael is here to get you dressed. I bet you're hungry and want some breakfast, too. After we have a good breakfast, we can play blocks. Do you want to play blocks with Uncle Michael?"

Little Maxwell nodded his head yes.

He was really enjoying his time with Maxwell and envied Todd, until he thought about how he treated Cynthia and Maxwell. Michael realized he couldn't be envious of someone who could hurt people he should love more than life itself.

CHAPTER 16

IT WASN'T UNTIL AFTER LUNCH that the hospital called to say Cynthia was able to go home.

"Let's go get your Mommy, Maxwell."

Maxwell was so excited. He was ready to run out the door without his shoes on.

"Wait until I put your shoes on, Maxwell. Can you find your shoes? We need our shoes on for outside."

Maxwell ran to the door to get shoes and brought them to Michael. He plunked himself down on the floor so Michael could put his shoes on him.

"Good job, Maxwell! Now we can go to the hospital to pick up Mommy."

When the two of them reached Cynthia's hospital room, Maxwell and Michael peeked around the door and saw her in a chair. Her left arm was in a sling. Cynthia looked up and saw two smiling faces looking at her.

She smiled at the sight of the two of them even though she was in quite a bit of pain. Her bruises were worse today, and she hoped it would not frighten Maxwell.

Maxwell pointed to her bruises and said, "Boo-boo."

Cynthia smiled and said, "Yes, sweetie. Lots of boo-boos, honey."

Sweet little Maxwell kissed her bruises.

Cynthia smiled at Maxwell and said, "Thank you, and, sweetie, they feel much better now." *If only it were so*, she thought.

As she looked at Maxwell, she wondered what would have happened to him if she had been killed in the accident. Even worse, it frightened her to think Maxwell might have been hurt or killed. He was everything to her.

"Was anyone able to get ahold of Todd?"

Michael just shook his head no.

Cynthia glanced away for a second as tears filled her eyes. Michael put his hand on Cynthia's hand because he saw her tears and knew what she was thinking.

The nurse walked in the room with the discharge papers for Cynthia to sign.

"Mrs. Marshall, the doctor will only agree to release you to go home if someone is able to stay with you for the next forty-eight hours. Will your husband be able to stay home with you?"

Cynthia hesitated for a moment. She knew the nurse probably thought Michael was her husband. Cynthia was about to cry. She just wanted to go home and be there with Maxwell. How could Todd leave her in this position? Before she could respond, Michael answered.

"No problem, Nurse. I'll be able to stay home with her."

He quickly signed his name where it said spouse or other signature.

Cynthia looked at Michael.

"Well, Maxwell, it looks like Mommy is going to be able to come home with us."

On the way home, Michael stopped at his place to get a clean outfit. When he finally reached their house, he carried Maxwell in one arm and put the other around Cynthia to help her inside the house and over to the couch. Once there, he gently placed pillows around her to make her comfortable and covered her with a blanket.

"I really appreciate you taking care of Maxwell and coming to pick me up, not to mention signing the papers so I could be released. I know I'll rest better now that I'm home, but it's not necessary for you to be bothered staying with us. You have done so much already in Todd's absence."

"I'm so sorry, but you heard the doctor's orders. Be a good patient! Besides, you need someone to take care of Maxwell. You're hardly able to take care of yourself, let alone him."

Cynthia just looked up at Michael and didn't say another word. She knew he was right. She didn't want him to miss work though, because they weren't his responsibility.

"What about missing work?"

"I haven't taken any time off of work for months, and this is as good of a reason as any. You don't want me to be diagnosed as a workaholic, do you? I don't think they have a cure for that yet. I guess I could always ask the doctor when I take you back to the hospital because there's no one to stay with you."

"Are you blackmailing me, Mr. Marshall?"

"Who, me? Never! Just stating the facts, madam."

"Michael, have you ever thought of being an attorney?"

All he could say was, "I rest my case."

CHAPTER 17

MICHAEL NOTICED THERE WASN'T MUCH in the house in the way of groceries. As soon as he got Maxwell down for his afternoon nap, he would make a quick trip to the store. Before he left, he made sure Cynthia was comfortable and the television was set for her soap operas, which were about to start.

Michael was hesitant about leaving them alone.

"Are you sure you're going to be okay by yourself?"

"I'll be fine, Michael. Maxwell is down for his nap, and I will remain right here until you get back. I promise."

"I will be back in a jiffy. It won't be any more than fifteen minutes. Here's something to drink and your cell phone, just in case you need me. Oh, I almost forgot. Here's a paper and pencil. Would you be able to take notes on the first soap opera so I won't miss any juicy details?"

This made Cynthia laugh.

"Michael, I didn't know you were crazy about soap."

"I certainly am. They're the highlight of my day. In fact, instead of taking notes, could you just call me on my cell phone if something exiting happens?"

Cynthia loved his sense of humor. A sense of humor was something that Todd definitely lacked.

"You are just too funny. You better watch it! I do know how to throw a punch, you know."

"I have heard that. On that note, I better leave quickly for the grocery store."

It was over twenty-four hours since the accident, and Cynthia still hadn't heard from Todd. She wondered why he wasn't answering his cell phone. If Maxwell had been hurt, wouldn't he like to know?

Days in the Lives of Our Families was about to start, and Cynthia was glad for the distraction to take her mind off of Todd and what he might be doing.

"Taylor, how could you do this to your own sister? I can't believe my own sister would hurt me like this by sleeping with my husband. Can't you find a man of your own? Do you have to take mine? I'm begging you to stay away from Steve so I can save my marriage."

"Your marriage can't be saved, Candace, and I can't take something that isn't yours anymore. He doesn't love you and hasn't for a long time. He loves me and wants me. So leave him alone like a good little girl."

Taylor pushed Candace in anger. Her sister fell backward against the end table, hitting her temple. Taylor waited for Candace to get up, but she lay unconscious and bleeding.

Cynthia felt sorry for Candace. Why couldn't Taylor just leave Steven alone? How could her sister cross the line and hurt her like that? None of her sisters would ever do that to her. Maybe not her sisters, but some no-good secretary might.

She didn't just blame Lucinda for what might be happening. It was Todd's fault for not loving her enough to remain faithful to her. Why couldn't he be more like Michael? Here she was injured, and who was the one there for her? Not Todd but Michael. She was through with Todd, and when she heard from him, she would let him know exactly how she felt.

Candace from *Days in the Lives of Our Families* should tell Steve she was through with him, she thought. Once a cheater, you can never trust him to be faithful. If it wasn't with Candace's sister, it would be with someone else.

On the TV, Taylor called 911 and prayed Candace would not die. This was not worth a life. All she wanted was for Candace to divorce Steven so they could be together. Why did this have to happen?

Michael was back in fifteen minutes.

"I'm back, Cynthia. I hurried as fast as I could because I didn't get a call about the soap."

"That's because it was so exciting I didn't want to miss anything by calling you. Sorry!"

"Oh, I see how it is. You just want to keep me in suspense."

"It was really exciting, too. You're just in time for *One Life to Give!*"

"Well, I'll just have to hurry and put the groceries away. Save me a seat!"

"Dina is a suitable kidney donor for Dora. If you are sure you want to go through with this, we need to have you sign the papers and get you immediately into surgery to do the transplant. Dora's kidneys are failing quickly."

"I am sure, Dr. Fred. Dora has to have this chance."

"Let's go then."

"I love you, Daddy!"

"I love you, Dina!"

During the surgery, Dr. Fred had a massive heart attack and died. His assistant was trying to keep Dora stable until another surgeon got scrubbed for the stat call.

Cynthia was so involved in the story it took her a minute to realize where the cackling laughter was coming from. As she turned her head toward the kitchen, she saw Michael ducking down out of sight. She began to laugh and flung the television guide over the counter with her good arm, knocking over Michael's plastic glass of water sitting on the counter.

Up popped Michael, soaked with water. She couldn't help but laugh at her soaked brother-in-law. She hadn't laughed this much in a long time. She couldn't help but reply to his antics with, "I guess justice is served!"

Michael walked over to the couch to give the guide back to Cynthia, apologizing for making fun of her soaps. He took her hand in his to call a truce. She looked so beautiful at that moment that he couldn't resist the temptation to lean down and kiss her.

CHAPTER 18

Cynthia and Michael held their kiss for what seemed like an eternity. It was full of more passion, intensity, and tenderness than either one had felt before.

At that moment, Cynthia's soap opera didn't matter. She had never been kissed like this before, even by Todd.

"I'm so sorry, Cynthia. I had no right to do that. It was completely out of line for me to take advantage of you under the circumstances. Please forgive me!"

"It's all right, Michael. You don't need to apologize. I know you would never take advantage of me. My marriage has not been good for a long time. I don't know when Todd stopped loving me or what I did for him not to love me, but I know there is nothing left of our marriage but a paper."

"You never could do anything to ruin your marriage. None of what has happened between you and Todd is your fault. You are a perfect wife and mother. Todd is stupid for not seeing that in you. I love you enough to know how loving you can be to your husband, child, and family."

"Michael, you said you love me?"

"I didn't mean to blurt that out. I just couldn't help it when I heard you blaming yourself. If I am being totally honest, I have been in love with you since before Todd and you were married. I just can't hide the way I feel about you. When I found Todd at Lucinda's, I couldn't hold back my anger and punched him in the nose. I don't know how my brother could be unfaithful to you. He doesn't deserve someone as wonderful as you."

"You have always been so caring, Michael. I thought long ago that Todd was caring and loving, but I was definitely blinded. Even before I was pregnant with Maxwell, I think Todd and I started drifting apart. Once I found out I was expecting, I thought the baby would help bring us back to the love we once shared. Unfortunately, it didn't happen. He can't even be a loving father to Maxwell, and that truly breaks my heart."

"No matter how things turn out, Cynthia, I promise I will help you through this."

"I know you will, Michael. I have known you long enough to know that you are a man of your word."

"I hope that I have the opportunity to show you how much I love you. Until then, I will not interfere with your marriage until you are certain it is truly over with Todd."

"Will you wait for me?"

"For as long as it takes!"

Michael felt so relieved to be able to tell Cynthia how he felt about her. He loved her so much that he wanted to yell it to the world, but he couldn't. Even though he couldn't, he knew Cynthia was worth waiting for, no matter how long it took.

Cynthia had tried not to be suspicious of Todd and Lucinda's late-night work meetings. She had trusted Todd because she loved him so much and she thought he still loved her. Finally, she now knew the truth about his escapades with Lucinda. She had made a big mistake thinking he was the one that would give her that fairy-tale marriage; instead, her marriage turned into a bad dream. Her sadness was not for herself but for Maxwell. Todd had never taken an interest in him since the day he was born, and he needed a father as much as he needed a mother.

CHAPTER 19

MAXWELL WAS WAKING UP FROM his nap, and Michael trotted up the stairs to get him from his crib. Michael peeked around the corner at Maxwell and said, "Peekaboo!" Maxwell giggled as Michael kept peeking around the corner, repeating "peekaboo" to him. Cynthia could hear Maxwell giggling and was enjoying Michael's interaction. She knew he would make a great father someday because he was always great with Maxwell.

Cynthia was glad Michael told her how he felt about her. She had never mentioned to anyone how she thought she had made a mistake marrying Todd, except Michael. She could now look to the future.

Michael and Maxwell giggled as they came down the stairs. The minute Michael put Maxwell down, he ran over to his mommy. He was trying to climb up on the couch beside her. Michael lifted him up gently next to Cynthia.

"Be very gentle with Mommy, Maxwell. Watch her booboos!"

Maxwell was as cute as he cuddled with her and patted her cheek softly. Cynthia couldn't have been happier, bruises and all, to be so well taken care of. As the two of them cuddled on the couch, Michael was in the kitchen cooking.

"What are you making? It smells so good," Cynthia asked.

"I am making my special homemade spaghetti sauce."

"When did you become such a good cook?"

"I guess when you're a bachelor, you need to cook or starve. I feel you enjoy the food so much more when you actually put some effort into it rather than pouring it out of a can. I do have to say I have become a pretty good chef over the years because I don't mind eating my own food. Also, I found out I have to put less on my plate to get filled up, but that could be because I taste the food quite often while I'm cooking it to make sure it's good."

"I'm sure if it is as good as it smells, we will definitely enjoy it. We love spaghetti. Don't we, Maxwell?"

"Sketti, yum," Maxwell replied.

When the spaghetti was finished, the three of them sat at the table enjoying every bite. They were almost finished with dinner when Todd walked in the door.

CHAPTER 20

"WELL, IF THIS ISN'T A pretty picture. Glad you're not missing me too much! So what's with all the urgent messages saying you were in a car accident? You look all right to me. I think you were just trying to get me to come home. I can't understand why! It looks like you're following after your son and having your own playdates. By the way, do your playdates come with sleepovers, too?"

Cynthia looked as though she was about to erupt but was trying to stay calm in front of Maxwell. Michael could see this was not going to be good, so he took Maxwell upstairs to give him a bath before bed.

As soon as Cynthia heard the bathroom door close, she didn't hesitate to react to his comments.

"Where have you been for the last two days, Todd? Having your playdate, as you call it, with Lucinda? You come in here and make accusations about your brother so you can try to relieve your guilt by accusing us of doing something wrong. Michael doesn't deserve that, nor do I. I have always been faithful to you, and that is more than I can say about you."

Cynthia had been watching Todd's expression on his face as she spoke up to him. She braced herself for his reaction because she knew it wasn't going to be nice.

"Hold on there, sweetness! I don't have to answer to you, little woman. Don't forget who keeps a roof over your head and supplies you with everything you need in life, including a child to occupy your time. Plus, I don't appreciate you trying to get me to come home by giving some lame excuse of being in an accident. Just because you call wolf doesn't mean I'm going to run home to you."

Cynthia could not hold back when she heard him say "lame excuse." If she could have jumped off the chair, she would have popped him in the nose again. She didn't have the energy to follow through with the idea. Lucky for him!

"You're saying it's a lame excuse! A car ran a red light and hit us. You didn't even have the decency to return any of the calls to see if your wife or child were all right? I want you to tell me where and what you were doing. No more of your lame excuses! I want the truth and not a bunch of lies. Were you really working on a big sales presentation with your secretary or was it a playdate?"

Todd was getting angry about her demands. She wanted the truth, and he was going to hold back. He was going to give her the hard truth and not sugarcoat it.

"I was with Lucinda, and we weren't working on a sales presentation. We were having a good time. Let me make that a wonderful time. Lucinda gives me all her attention, and that is what I want from my woman. That is something you never give me. Frankly, I am fed up with a woman who promised to be a wife. You're not living up to what you vowed, so I had to find it elsewhere, and that is your fault. So you go ahead and continue your playdate with Michael."

"That is really nice, Todd. You bring up our wedding vows and how this is all my fault. All those late nights, I believed you were telling me the truth about working on those so-called sales presentations, when all the time you were sleeping with Lucinda. Spending time with her instead of Maxwell, your son, and your wife. I see how you feel about our marriage, but what about Maxwell? Don't you care about your son?"

Todd had already said so many hurtful things, but the worst comment was yet to come.

"I don't even think Maxwell is my son. From the looks of what I have just interrupted, I probably know who his daddy is. Unless there is someone else or others you have been spending your time with while I was away."

Cynthia couldn't believe Todd could even think, let alone say, such a thing. She didn't care about him being with Lucinda at this point or that he didn't think she was giving her full attention to him. For him to even think Maxwell wasn't his was ludicrous. How could he accuse Michael of being the father? Cynthia had never been with anyone else. At that moment, Cynthia was glad Michael had gone upstairs to give Maxwell his bath. If Todd had said these things to her with Michael in the room, she knew he would have decked Todd. She was through with Todd—absolutely through!

"Enough of your accusations and demeaning statements, Todd. Just because you are an adulterer with your slutty secretary doesn't mean I would ever lower myself to your standards. If you want to take a paternity test to prove Maxwell is yours, then let's do it. You may have helped with his conception, but you never have been a father to him. You don't even know what you're missing. So get out of here and don't come back!"

"Well, look who is finally showing her true self. I knew behind that quiet, unexciting personality, someday you would show your true self. Maybe you thought acting the way you did was likeable, but I thought it was terribly boring. Now that I see you are showing yourself to be a little spitfire, maybe I'll change my mind and keep you."

Michael was coming down the stairs after putting Maxwell to bed. He looked over at Cynthia as she picked up her coffee cup and flung it at Todd, hitting him with perfect precision directly in the nose.

Todd was caught off guard because he was looking over at the stairs. After the cup hit his nose, he stumbled backward, almost falling over. With one look at Michael, Todd grabbed his aching nose and escaped out the door in fear Michael might throw a punch at him, too.

CHAPTER 21

MICHAEL GRINNED AT CYNTHIA, WHO looked as though she were ready to bawl when Todd slammed the door. He was glad she had stood up to Todd and didn't let him convince her she was at fault for any of what had transpired.

"Great aim!" Michael said. "I guess you don't need me to help put Todd in his place, especially in your weakened condition!"

Cynthia couldn't help but laugh. Michael could always find a way to make her laugh in a tense situation.

"Help? Who me? You know that felt really good," she said, knowing she had finally taken a stand with Todd. She was glad she had, for both herself and Maxwell. It had been a long time coming, and this was a perfect time to do it.

Michael helped Cynthia to the couch and sat down beside her. He had heard everything Todd had said, including not thinking Maxwell was his son. There was no way Cynthia would ever be disloyal to Todd. He felt sorry for Cynthia that Todd had said such hateful things. If he hadn't been upstairs putting Maxwell to bed, he would have let his brother have more than a cup in his already broken nose.

He looked at Cynthia, and more than anything he wanted to hold her in his arms to show her how he felt about her, but it was not an appropriate time. She was very vulnerable, and Michael didn't want to take advantage of her. He wanted Cynthia to want him—and not just because she was so angry with Todd.

Michael looked at Cynthia's soft pink lips and remembered how wonderful they felt against his. The thought of kissing her excited him. It was hard to hold back because he wanted to show her how much he loved her. He had to be patient. Until that time, he would be there for her and Maxwell. He would always be there for them, no matter what happened, even if it didn't include him.

Soon she would be well enough to take care of Maxwell and he would be going back to his house. The thought of this made him sad because being with them every day gave him great joy.

CHAPTER 22

CYNTHIA HAD A PRETTY RESTFUL night's sleep that night. She was so grateful Michael had offered to take care of Maxwell and be there for her. She knew she could not have taken care of him, let alone herself. As she lay there resting, she could hear Michael talking to Maxwell while he dressed him. Michael was so great with Maxwell; in fact, Michael was great in every way. Just as she was coming out of her room, Michael was coming out with Maxwell.

"There's your mommy! We thought Mommy was still sleeping. Didn't we?" Michael said.

"Good morning, my sweet Maxwell and Uncle Michael. Did Uncle Michael get you dressed for breakfast for Mommy?"

Maxwell nodded yes.

"You have a kiss for Mommy?" Maxwell bent forward and kissed her on the lips. "Thank you! You sure know how to make Mommy feel better."

Michael switched Maxwell to his other arm. "Let me help you downstairs, Cynthia."

He guided her to the couch where she would be more comfortable while he and Maxwell made breakfast. The two of them were deciding what to have for breakfast when the phone rang.

"Don't get up, Cynthia! I'll grab the phone."

It was Cynthia's sister Marie. She was a nurse at Cleary Medical Center in the ICU department. She had just finished up with three twelve-hour shifts. Now she had the next two days off.

"Who was that on the phone?"

"It was Marie. She is coming over to visit you in a little while. She wants to see how you are doing from the car accident. If you want, I can take Maxwell to the park to play while the two of you visit."

"I would appreciate that, Michael, and I am sure Maxwell would love to go to the park to play."

She was glad Michael wanted to take Maxwell to play at the park. He needed sometime outside to play, and she really was feeling some pain today.

Cynthia was excited Marie was coming over. Marie was married to Vincent Riley, a chemist. When Marie and Vincent got married, their plan was to wait three years before starting their family. For five years they had been trying to have a baby and were beginning to lose all hope of having the family they wanted.

Vincent came from a family of four brothers and three sisters. He was the oldest of eight children. He was really looking forward to their own children, especially now since he had many nieces and nephews from his siblings.

Marie was excited to be able to spend some time with Cynthia. The minute she came in the door, she was checking Cynthia's bruises, her arm, and asking her what pain level she was experiencing. Michael knew that Cynthia was in good hands and decided it was a great time to go to the park with Maxwell.

"All right, Marie! Remember you are off work. I'm fine, except for a few bruises."

"What is Michael doing here taking care of you and Maxwell? Where is Todd?"

"I will explain everything, Marie. No one was able to get in touch with Todd after the accident. My loving husband, if you can call Todd that, was getting the messages but happened to be too preoccupied to take the call."

"I'm not following you, Cynthia. What was he preoccupied doing?"

"Todd finally did come home last night. He accused me of making the accident up to get him to come home. As to what he was doing ... he was with Lucinda ... working late ... make that very late. At least that is always how he would describe it to me, which really meant being unfaithful to his loving wife."

"You can't be serious! Todd?"

"Yes, that's the one."

"I can't believe he would do that to you."

"I never wanted to believe it either, Marie. I was so madly in love with him and believed so much in the happily-ever-after thing. I thought no one could ever tear us apart. All those times he told me he was working late with Lucinda were lies. He said Lucinda was giving him the attention he wanted from his woman."

"I am so sorry, Cynthia. I can't believe Todd would do this to you. I thought you two would be together forever."

Marie could see the tears in her sister's eyes. She reached over and gently gave her sister a hug.

"I'm sorry to say this, Cynthia, but I never trusted Todd."

"Why not?"

"I never told you this because I didn't want to hurt you and didn't think you would even believe me. He said once you two were married, we would all be family, and he wanted to know me better. I told him never to put his hands on me again. He told me if I said anything to you, he would tell you I tried to kiss him. He said you would believe him because you were crazy in love with him."

"I was crazy in love with Todd. He had me under such a spell I might not have believed you, and I'm sorry for that. I thought he would move mountains to make me happy, but all he cares about is his own happiness. There is no way the hospital would have let me come home if I didn't have someone to stay with Maxwell and me. Since Todd hasn't returned any messages we sent to him, Michael offered to stay with us. He is there for us, not Todd."

Marie wasn't surprised Michael had helped. She knew before Todd and Cynthia were married that Michael was in love with Cynthia. The only thing good out of her marriage to Todd was Maxwell. Marie hoped someday she would have a child as sweet as him.

More than anything, she wanted to give Vincent children, especially a son. As happy as they were, their marriage would not be complete until they had children. Her biological clock was ticking, and she needed to conceive soon to be able to have the family they wanted.

Marie was glad Cynthia opened up to her about everything. It was hard to hear that Cynthia's dream marriage was over, but she knew her sister would find happiness with someone else. She had a feeling it might be with Michael.

As Marie was preparing lunch for Cynthia, Michael and Maxwell came back from the playground. Maxwell must have been tuckered out, as he was fast asleep in Michael's arms as he carried him upstairs while gently rubbing his back.

When Michael came downstairs, Marie offered to make him some lunch, but they had stopped for something to eat after the playground.

"Thanks anyway, Marie. You ladies have a good time, but I need to run home. I'll be back soon so I don't miss too much of the soap operas."

After Michael walked out the door, Marie asked, "Cynthia, is he just playing with us about watching the soaps?"

"Sure! He just has a great sense of humor."

"Maybe he just wants to spend a little time with a certain someone, if you catch my drift."

"Yes, I do catch your drift, but right now I need to deal with Todd. So, say no more because the soaps are about to start."

Cynthia caught Marie up on the details of *Days in the Lives of Our Families* while the commercials were on.

"Taylor and Candace are arguing over Steven. Taylor pushes Candace, and she falls off balance, hitting her head on the end table. Candace is laying on the floor unconscious and bleeding. Taylor calls 911."

They watched as Candace was taken by ambulance to the hospital, and the police were questioning Taylor as to how her sister got hurt.

"It was an accident. We were just having a little argument. I didn't mean to hurt her. Please, I beg you to let me go to the hospital. I need to be with my sister. This is just a terrible accident."

"At this time, we aren't going to press any charges against you until we can get a statement from Mrs. Bradford when she regains consciousness."

Taylor called Steven as she drove to the hospital to tell him about Candace being hurt.

"Steven, it's Taylor. There's been a terrible accident."

"Taylor, are you hurt?"

"I wasn't in an accident, Steven. It's Candace. We were arguing. I didn't mean to push hard, but she must have lost her balance. She fell backward and hit her head on the end table. She is unconscious, and the ambulance is taking her to the ER. Please meet me there!"

"I'll leave right away. She's going to be all right, Taylor. Don't worry!"

When the two of them got to the hospital, the doctors were examining Candace and sending her for a CT scan. It was a little over an hour before Candace got to a room. The doctor walked over to Steven with the results.

"Are you Mr. Bradford?"

"Yes, I am."

"I'm Doctor Moore. I'm your wife's doctor. May I talk to you privately about your wife?"

"This is Candace's sister, Taylor. It's all right to talk about Candace in front of her. She is very concerned about her sister."

"Yes, Mr. Bradford. The tests show there is no skull fracture or permanent damage, but she is still in a coma. Your baby is all right as well."

"I didn't know my wife was pregnant. How far along is she, Doctor?"

"She is a little over two months. There is some minor spotting, but everything looks good, and we will keep monitoring her."

"Thank you, Dr. Moore. We appreciate it."

"Oh my God, Steven, what have I done? Candace could have lost the baby. I could have killed Candace."

Marie and Cynthia were shocked when they heard Candace was pregnant.

"Who do you think the father is, Cynthia?"

"It has to be Steven. He really looked surprised though."

"I guess even in soap operas you can get pregnant. Why can't that be true in real life?"

Cynthia looked at Marie and saw tears in her eyes.

"It will happen, Marie. When it does, you will make a terrific mother, and Vincent will be a terrific father. Just don't give up hope!"

Marie didn't want to give up hope, but every month when her period came, she was so disappointed. Maybe she needed to not be so stressed about it and let nature take its course.

When *Days in the Lives of Our Families* was over, Cynthia quickly filled Marie in with the latest details of *One Life to Give*.

"They just have found out Dina is a match for the kidney transplant for Dora. During the surgery, Dr. Fred has a massive heart attack and dies. They are trying to keep Dora stable while Dr. Ferris is scrubbing to take over the kidney transplant."

Cynthia and Marie were so involved in their story they didn't hear Michael come back. He couldn't resist saying, "Boo!" Both Marie and Cynthia jumped.

"Michael Marshall, you scared Cynthia and me nearly have to death."

Michael couldn't stop laughing. Marie picked up a pillow and threw it at him.

"Michael, tell us the truth! You are teasing us because you really want to know what's happening with Dina. You love watching the soaps as much as we do, but you are just afraid to admit it," Cynthia said.

"Poor Michael! Come sit down with us. We will share the excitement. We don't want you to miss out on the stories."

Michael smiled and sat down between the two of them.

The minute the soap opera came back on, Dora's family members were all crying.

Michael pretended he was sobbing, too. They both looked at him and started tickling him. He was having a great time pretending he was captivated with the saga.

"The patient's heart rate is dropping. Get the crash cart! Come on, Dora. Hang on. Don't you die on us now!"

Michael blurted out, "It's over! How will I ever be able to sleep tonight not knowing if Dora is going to survive?"

Cynthia and Marie just shook their heads as Michael went upstairs to get Maxwell.

"Cynthia, I have to get home to Vincent. I don't want him to think I have been having fun all day watching soap operas. I had such a good time, and I know I am leaving you in good hands with Michael taking care of you."

Marie was on her way out of the door when she turned around to Cynthia and said, "He is so dramatic. I always knew that man was a keeper. You break it off with Todd, you should marry Michael—or at least keep him for your ... man servant."

Cynthia smiled. Just as Michael was coming down the stairs with Maxwell, Cynthia said, "Man servant! I like those words a lot."

Cynthia looked over at Michael, and he was smiling at her but didn't say a word. She just laughed.

CHAPTER 23

ON THE DRIVE HOME, MARIE thought about what Todd had done to Cynthia and the terrible things he had said to her. Now she wished she had warned Cynthia about Todd; maybe she could have changed her sister's mind about marrying him. It might have saved her sister the pain of having an adulterer husband.

Todd had seemed to be so crazy about Cynthia; no one would have ever thought he was the kind to sleep around. He had been so patient, waiting for their marriage to have sex with her. She wanted to wait until marriage, and he said he understood. Maybe it didn't bother him to wait for her if he was getting what he wanted from another woman—or maybe women.

Knowing she had been a virgin, how could he even suspect Maxwell was anyone else's but his? To even think Maxwell was not his was despicable. Cynthia would never have been unfaithful. She would have done anything to make him happy, but apparently that wasn't good enough for him.

It was evident now that Cynthia had married the wrong brother. Michael was terrific with Maxwell. Someday he would be a terrific father. He had shown more kindness to Maxwell and Cynthia than Todd ever had or could.

Annie's husband, Charlie, was terrific with their twins, Annabelle and Andy. He helped raise the twins as much as Annie did. Annie said she would never have been able to take care of twins if it were not for Charlie being such a great father.

Marie's heart ached, longing to have Vincent's children. They were ready to start their family, and nothing was happening. She wondered if they had waited too long.

CHAPTER 24

M ICHAEL STAYED WITH CYNTHIA FOR close to three days. He not only took care of Maxwell and cared for Cynthia, but he also cooked and kept up with the wash. He was so happy to be there for her and to spend time with Maxwell. He would greatly miss his time there.

She was so grateful he had been there to help with Maxwell. She could not have taken care of him. Michael had done a terrific job, something she knew Todd could not have done.

Cynthia was sorry she had married Todd, thinking he was Mr. Right. She still couldn't believe what happened between the two of them. It would be embarrassing for everyone to know Todd didn't want her and turned to someone else. She had told everyone he was the perfect man and how much they loved each other. The truth was he didn't love her nearly as much as she loved him.

Their marriage vows said to honor each other and until death. These words apparently meant nothing to Todd. What a fool she was to think her happily-ever-after was going to be with him. How wrong she had been to think he was the person for her.

How angry she was that she had wasted her life with him as well as her virginity. Lucinda could have him, and soon she would see how he tired of her, and she would not be enough.

Ken and Lorraine would be back soon from vacation. Cynthia wondered how they would react when they found out what Todd had done. She loved his parents and cared dearly about them. He would have to be the one to explain to them why his marriage was over. No matter what, she hoped they would still be there for Maxwell. They idolized Todd, and what happened would break their hearts.

She thought about her parents and how she wasn't looking forward to telling them about what Todd had done. There had never been a divorce in the Cleary family. Hers was going to be the first.

CHAPTER 25

The two weeks Ken and Lorraine had spent in Hawaii had gone by quickly. The weather was perfect, and the ocean was a mesmerizing blue that was overwhelming. It was a relaxing vacation, and they thoroughly enjoyed being there.

Even though they had a great time, they couldn't wait to see their little grandson, Maxwell. They just had to stop on the way home and give him a big hug. They reminded him so much of their precious Todd at that age. Just as smart as his daddy, and they knew he would be just as successful.

They were hoping Maxwell was not down for his nap so they would be able to visit with him. When they opened the door, there was sweet little Maxwell sitting on the floor playing with his toys.

Maxwell heard the door open and looked up to see his grandma and grandpa.

"Gammy, Gammpy!" Maxwell exclaimed as he ran over to them.

"Hi, pumpkin. We've missed you so much," they harmonized while they flooded him with hugs and kisses.

"Mom, Dad … I'll be right there. I am just getting Maxwell's lunch together. How was your vacation? Did you have a good time?" Cynthia asked.

"Every day was absolutely perfect. It was a wonderful, relaxing vacation and very romantic," Lorraine said.

"You just can't believe how beautiful the ocean is there and so calm. The sunsets and sunrises are something to see. I can't even describe how beautiful. The three of you are just going to have to take a vacation to Hawaii. Maxwell would enjoy playing in the water and building sandcastles," Ken added.

Cynthia walked from the kitchen to Ken and Lorraine.

"Cynthia, honey, what the heck happened to you?" Lorraine asked.

"I'm all right, Mom. Don't fret! I was coming home from my sisters with Maxwell, and a car decided to run a red light. It was almost a week ago. I'm much better now. Fortunately, Maxwell was not hurt at all."

"For heaven's sake, these people who try making it through red lights drive me crazy. Lucky for you, you weren't both killed, and Maxwell wasn't hurt," Ken added.

"Yes, I agree, Dad. I was worried about Maxwell when I woke up in the hospital. He was not hurt, and that was a blessing to me."

"Do you want us to take Maxwell home for a few days so you can rest, darling?" asked Lorraine.

"I appreciate it, Mom, but I look a lot worse than I am feeling."

Cynthia wanted to add, "Especially since Michael was here to take care of us because your precious son Todd was too busy with other extracurricular activities." She thought it best she didn't say anything. Todd should be the one to tell them about his indiscretions.

Everything seemed to go well with the visit of Todd's parents. They left after Maxwell ate his lunch so he could go down for his nap. As they were on the way out of the house, they told Cynthia if she changed her mind about them taking care of Maxwell to call them, and they added for her to tell Todd they were back from Hawaii.

Cynthia was relieved when they left. Not because she didn't love them but because she didn't want to have to explain about Todd and Lucinda. She couldn't help but wonder what kind of relationship she would have with them once they knew the truth. Would they side with him?

Never in her wildest dreams had she thought that they would have to hear about marriage problems with Todd and her.

Even thinking about it made her sick to her stomach. It was finally sinking in—what the two of them had done to her marriage. This broke her heart not only because what they did hurt her but also because other family members would be hurt because of their actions.

Why did this happen? What did she do to cause Todd to break their vows? How would this affect Maxwell? Would Todd's parents hate her?

CHAPTER 26

"IT SURE IS NICE TO be home," said Lorraine.

"It is nice, but I do miss that soft, sandy beach and beautiful blue Hawaiian ocean. I don't think it would be hard for me to turn into a beach bum."

"I wouldn't mind it either if the kids were all in Hawaii, too."

"Little Maxwell is such a joy. I don't know what we would do without him in our life. Every time we see him, he seems to have grown so much."

"He is something else. Don't you think he is the spitting image of his daddy at that age, Ken?"

"He definitely is. No doubt about that. I don't know about you, Lorraine, but I am a bit exhausted from the flight home."

"I am, too. Well there is all the time difference and long flight. It always does seem longer coming home from a vacation than going to the destination. Why don't we wait for a while before we unpack and start washing out clothes?"

"Sounds like a terrific idea to me!"

"Ken, I am so upset over Cynthia being in a car accident while we were gone. I wish Todd would have called us to let us know. Even when are away having fun, we do think about them."

"No, Lorraine, you would have been so worried, and there wouldn't have been anything we could have done being that far away. You probably would have wanted to catch the first flight back home. Except for Cynthia having some bruises, she seems to be all right. Maxwell is fine, so stop your fretting and relax."

"I know you're right, Ken. I can't imagine how frightened Maxwell must have been. The whole thing just terrifies me, thinking our little grandson might have been hurt or even killed."

"Now, honey, don't go thinking *what if*. He is fine, and we should be thankful for the fact he is safe, and so is Cynthia."

"I am thankful, Ken. You know me, the worry wart though."

"Yes I do, but even though you are a worry wart, I love every little inch of you."

"I love you more, Ken."

"I have an idea you can use all that worrying energy on. Why don't you make plans for a picnic with all the kids? Tell Michael and Ben to even bring a date. The more the merrier!"

"How did I get so lucky to have you for a husband? You do know how to cheer me up."

"I do my best, Lorraine. I'll do anything to make you happy, sweetie."

"Ken, that is exactly why I have stayed married to you for so many years. Of course, the main reason is the fact I am crazy in love with you."

"I know, Lorraine. Perhaps we should take the luggage upstairs and rest up there where it is quiet."

"Ken Marshall, I can see right through you. Because it is quieter is not the reason you want to go upstairs."

"I am thinking of your physical well-being, honey."

"Of course you are, Ken. I really appreciate your concern, too."

Ken always had a way of cheering Lorraine up. She loved his sense of humor. Their marriage had always been wonderful. She had never regretted marrying him. The had a wonderful life together and raised three sons who they loved so much.

They had always been proud of their sons' accomplishments and the fact that Todd brought Cynthia into their family. Cynthia was a terrific wife and mother.

Todd and Cynthia had given them their first grandchild. Hopefully there would be many more grandchildren to come. Their hope was that Ben and Michael would fall in love and start having their own families.

Ken and Lorraine were not excited Ben chose to be a cop. A cop didn't make a lot of money to support his family. There was also the concern he might get hurt or even killed. They knew he wanted a family and prayed he would find a woman that was not afraid of being married to a cop. Too bad he didn't want to be an architect like Michael or work as a sales rep for a pharmaceutical company like Todd.

Of their two unmarried sons, Michael was the one ready to fall in love and start a family. He was terrific with Maxwell. He hoped he would someday find a woman who was like Cynthia—a good wife and mother. Michael had told his parents that Todd didn't realize how lucky he was to have found Cynthia. They hoped someday soon Michael would find a Cynthia of his own to love and have children with.

CHAPTER 27

Todd had a good day at work and was anxious to tell Lucinda about the big account he signed. Before he told her though, he wanted to tell his parents. They were always so proud of all his accomplishments and how he well he provided for his family. Todd knew they had just gotten back from their vacation in Hawaii and wanted to hear all about the trip.

The signs of his broken nose were still very much evident, and he wasn't quite sure how he would explain it. If they found out how it happened, he would just tell them Cynthia wasn't the wonderful wife and mother they thought she was. None of what happened was his fault.

He pulled in his parents' driveway and sat there for a minute, trying to decide what to tell them. After building up enough courage, he walked in the house ready to give them an explanation.

"Mom and Dad, where are you?"

"Todd, is that you? We're out here on the patio relaxing."

"Relaxing? I thought you just got back from vacation."

"We did, but now we're resting from our resting. Vacation can take a lot out of you. We stopped at your place on the way home from the airport because we just had to see Maxwell. Didn't Cynthia tell you … and what the heck happened to you?"

"Mom, I'm on the mend. Don't go getting yourself excited. It's much better than it was, I assure you. Cynthia's temper got the worst of her, and she threw something at me. I can say one thing about her: she knows how to throw. Maybe I should have her go to tryouts for a baseball team and see if they will take her on as pitcher. She could make us some money instead of sitting around watching soaps all the time."

"I can't believe Cynthia would be violent like that toward you. It just seems out of character for her," said Ken.

"She never even mentioned anything to us when we stopped at your house. Not that it is any of our business when you two have a little squabble," added Lorraine.

"Sweet little Cynthia is not the woman I thought she was when I married her. The kid has really changed her. It wasn't just a squabble either. She downright kicked me out of my own house. I give her everything, and still I'm not good enough in her eyes."

"Todd, every husband and wife have times they fight, but that doesn't mean she doesn't love you. Maybe she just needs to cool off a little bit. Just go home and tell her you're sorry. Women like that kind of thing. That is all she needs to hear, and then things will be all right," Ken advised his son.

"It doesn't make a difference what I do, Dad. She isn't the Cynthia you know. Maybe she would be if Michael would stay away from her. He is over there, and the three of them are playing like one big happy family."

"Now, Todd, I can't believe Michael or Cynthia would ever do that to you. Maybe you're mistaken about all of this because you're upset," said Lorraine.

"I walked in on them playing house, Mom. You know how Michael is always looking at Cynthia with his lovesick eyes. The way he fusses over Maxwell, you would think he is his father. For all I know, maybe Michael is his father."

"This whole thing is just awful, Todd. I am so angry at Michael and Cynthia for doing this to you and Maxwell. Cynthia never mentioned any of this to us when we stopped to see them. She didn't even act like there was anything wrong between the two of you. I'm so sorry all this is happening to you, Todd," Lorraine sympathized with her son.

"Mom, do you honestly think she would admit to either one of you she is not the wonderful wife and mother you thought her to be? She fooled me, too. I thought she loved me more than anything, and now look what she's done to our marriage."

"Well, your father and I will be making it a priority to have a long talk with Michael about this whole mess. There will be no more of him interfering with your marriage after Dad gets finished talking with him. This really upsets us."

"Sorry I had to break the bad news to you, especially when I really came over to tell you about the big account I brought in today. It will mean a great big bonus for me. I was just so excited, and you two are the only ones that care about how hard I work."

"We are so proud of you and all you have achieved to be able to give your family everything they could possibly need. After your mother and I talk to Michael, he will be staying away from Cynthia and Maxwell. Give it some time, and maybe you can forgive Cynthia for what she has done. For your son's sake, you need to keep this marriage together."

"I don't know if that is possible, Dad, after what the two of them have done to me. This really hurt me a lot. I really appreciate the two of you being on my side. In the meantime, I'm staying over at Lucinda's. She is terrific and appreciates my accomplishments. Cynthia is nothing like her. I've worked my but off to give Cynthia everything, and she's done this to me."

"Of course we would be on your side, Todd. There is never any excuse for infidelity. Family is the most important thing. Everything will be okay, Todd. We're so proud of you and always will be. Trust your dad and me!"

"I will, Mom. I know you and Dad always stick by me. Lucinda is the same way. She has been there to support me in everything I do. I'm on the way over to see her now. She will be happy to hear I closed the new account earlier than I expected."

Todd was excited to tell Lucinda. They would be sharing a bottle of champagne that night.

CHAPTER 28

K EN AND LORRAINE WERE UPSET Michael had come between
Cynthia and Todd. How could he hurt his brother like this?
Something needed to be done before things got worse. Cynthia and
Todd needed to save their marriage. Hopefully, Todd would forgive
Cynthia for Maxwell's sake.

The two of them had such a nice vacation in Hawaii, and they
weren't too happy to come home to this mess. Their plans of getting
everyone together were now canceled. They didn't want to have a get-
together with Todd and Michael fighting over Cynthia.

Lorraine asked Ken to call Michael and ask him to come over. She
cautioned him to talk with Michael about the incident and not yell at
him. They loved Michael, but this was unacceptable behavior from any
of their sons whom they taught to have better values.

Ken called Michael and asked him to stop over when he had a free
minute. He was glad Michael said he would come over right away.

When Ken and Lorraine heard Michael drive up, Lorraine went
upstairs so Ken and Michael could have privacy to discuss what was
happening with Cynthia.

"Hi, Dad. How was your trip?"

"We had a great time. Nothing like getting away from everything.
We were looking forward to coming home, but now I'm not so sure."

"What do you mean? Where's Mom? Is she all right?"

"Your mother is fine. That is not why I asked you to come over,
Michael. I thought the two of us could have a man-to-man talk. Let me
explain before you say anything. Michael, when we raised you boys, we
tried to teach you good moral values. We hoped when you grew up, you
would adhere to those values."

"Dad, what are you talking about?"

"Hold on, son! Let me finish what I have to say. Todd stopped by just after we got home. Apparently, you have been interfering with Todd's marriage."

"What exactly does that mean … interfering?"

"I think a long time ago we had the talk about the birds and the bees. This time, Cynthia is the bee, and you're the bird. From what your mom and I understand from Todd, you are the one getting the honey."

"Are you saying Todd told you Cynthia and I are involved?"

"His words were … you were playing house with Cynthia. I don't think you mother and I needed an interpretation of what he meant by playing house."

"Where is Mom?"

"Your mom wants us to talk about this Michael."

"Dad … what I am going to say to you needs to be heard by Mom, too."

"Michael, your mom is upset enough over what you and Cynthia have been doing without getting her in on this discussion."

"This discussion is built on a bunch of lies. Now, have Mom come down here or I will go up there and get her!"

"Lorraine, can you come down here! Michael wants to talk to both of us."

Lorraine came downstairs with some hesitation. She didn't like to talk to her sons about sexual issues. This was something they needed to discuss with their father.

"All right, Michael, what do you want your father and me to hear?"

"Todd has been feeding you both a bunch of lies, and you both need to know the truth."

"So tell your father and me your version of the truth!"

"First of all, I was over at their house taking care of Maxwell after Cynthia was released from the hospital. Todd was nowhere to be found."

"What do you mean he couldn't be found? Plus, what does this have to do with you and Cynthia having an affair?" Ken asked Michael.

"Dad, we weren't and are not having an affair. Ben and I were looking for Todd when Cynthia was hurt. The reason we couldn't find him was because he was away having a romantic rendezvous weekend with Lucinda."

"Don't try and defend yourself by accusing Todd," said Lorraine.

"Mom … I stopped over at Todd's one evening before the accident. Todd canceled out on supper because he said he had to work on a sales promotion with Lucinda; at least that is how he described his late night to Cynthia. Cynthia was in tears, so I went to Jenson's to talk with Todd. When he wasn't there, I tried Lucinda's. When Lucinda opened the door, she was in her robe, and Todd was in the bedroom. My sister-in-law's unfaithful husband was in his undershorts in Lucinda's bed. I don't think they were discussing some big pharmaceutical business matter. I was so angry with him I punched him in the nose and broke it. When Cynthia was hurt in the car accident, I stayed there because she could only be released if someone could stay with her and take care of Maxwell. There was nothing else going on between Cynthia and me. I have too much respect for her to cross that line. Todd is the one who is fooling around, not Cynthia."

"I don't understand why Todd would lie to your father and me or why Cynthia didn't say something to us about Todd."

"Todd knows you two will believe anything he says because he can do no wrong in your eyes. Cynthia didn't feel it was her place to tell you about Todd and Lucinda. She is such a kind woman she wouldn't want you to think badly of Todd, but I don't care."

"We are so sorry, Michael. We were misled by Todd. I don't understand why he would make up such a story about the two of you, but we certainly will have a talk with him," Ken said.

"I am sorry you two had to come home to this, Dad. I assure both of you, Cynthia would never break her wedding vows. She is the perfect wife and mother. Any man would be proud to have a wife like her. God know I would."

"It was easy for us to believe Todd because we have always known how you feel about Cynthia and Maxwell. When you love someone so deeply, it is hard to disguise your feelings. We are asking you to please not interfere with your brother's marriage if they can patch things up. Will you please do that for us, Michael?" asked his mother.

"I didn't know it showed how I feel about Cynthia and Maxwell. I promise both of you I will stay out of their marriage as long as Cynthia wants to make it work. Todd is hurting Cynthia terribly. I just couldn't bear seeing Todd hurt her any more, and that is why I went to find him. She doesn't deserve that."

"Michael, we are so sorry for Cynthia and what Todd has done to her. We will be discussing this with him and why he lied to us. He must stop his affair with Lucinda and try to reconcile with Cynthia for Maxwell's sake," said Ken.

"Mom and Dad, I want Cynthia to be happy, so I promise you I will not interfere. On the other hand, if I ever find out he is hurting her in any way, I cannot promise you I will not interfere."

"Dad and I will hold you to that promise."

CHAPTER 29

T ODD STOPPED AT THE BEVERAGE store on the way to Lucinda's to get a bottle of champagne. He knew they would be partying tonight because of his good news. Lucinda sure knew how to party, and that was something Cynthia would never do.

Lucinda was probably in the bedroom, so he quietly walked in the door to surprise her. He jumped in front of the bedroom door, yelling, "Champagne anyone?"

There was his perfect woman, Lucinda, lying in bed, but she was not alone. He knew exactly who was with her when he saw the bald head.

"Lucinda, what the heck is going on here? I just closed one of my biggest accounts yet, and you're making it with Doug Mills in bookkeeping?"

"Todd baby, I'm so sorry!"

"Sorry? Sorry doesn't cut it, Lucinda. We had a good thing going, but apparently it wasn't good enough for you."

"Todd baby, it just happened. This isn't anything."

"Well you can just continue with your 'isn't anything,' as you call, it with Mills because I am leaving and taking this expensive bottle of champagne out of here. You just lost the best thing you've ever had in your life, Lucinda. I hope it's worth it to have a roll in the sack with this scumbag Mills."

"Don't call me a scumbag, Marshall!"

"You stay out of this, Mills, before I pound you to a pulp. This is one of the biggest days of my life, and you ruined it, Lucinda. We're done!"

"Todd baby, please wait! Don't leave, please! It will never happen again. You always tell me I'm the best you've ever had. Cynthia is nothing. You even said it yourself. Please tell me you'll forgive me, Todd!"

Lucinda heard the door slam. She knew she had made a mistake with Mills. Todd was angrier than she had ever seen him. He just had to forgive her. This couldn't be the end of what Todd and she had. It just couldn't be!

CHAPTER 30

TODD SAT IN HIS CAR wondering what to do. He couldn't believe Lucinda would have the audacity to cheat on him with a bookkeeper. Mills made a fraction of the amount of money he made. How could Mills ever give her the lifestyle Todd could give her? Why would she even be interested in that baldheaded eagle? He couldn't even afford to take her to a decent restaurant.

He felt betrayed by Lucinda. She had always been there for him in his climb up the ladder to being one of the best salesmen. He always thought he was her main concern, until now. Here he was with an expensive bottle of champagne and no one to share it with. The worst part of this mess with Lucinda was, where was he going to stay?

The only thing he could think to do was go back home. He couldn't just walk in the front door and yell, "I need a place to stay." He would have to work his charm on Cynthia. She couldn't know Lucinda was fooling around on him. He always had a way with words, and this time his story had to be really convincing.

Todd drove to his house and parked down the street to get his story straight before he walked in the door. When he was ready, he got out of his car in the driveway and popped the cork on the champagne bottle. Todd took some big chugs of the bubbly drink and poured some of it over the front of his shirt.

Maxwell would be in bed by now, so Todd would have Cynthia's full attention. His plan was to make her think he made a mistake and he couldn't live without her. She wasn't exactly what he wanted, but at least she was someone to have sex with until he found someone else to satisfy his loins.

He placed the key in the door lock and turned it, getting ready for his entrance.

"Cynthia, I need to talk with you. Where are you, honey?"

"Todd, I'm in the kitchen. Be quiet or you'll wake Maxwell. What do you want?"

"I want you, baby."

Todd walked toward the kitchen table and bumped into a chair, which added some special effects to his supposed drunkenness. Stumbling, he landed on the floor at Cynthia's feet. He got to his knees and placed his hands on her lap as he tried to fondle her.

"Todd, I don't know what you think you're doing, but it isn't going to work with me."

"Cynthia, I can't live without you. You know I love you, and I know you still love me. We belong together. My heart aches for you."

"Todd, you're drunk. Why don't you go home to your perfect Lucinda? You wanted her, remember?"

"I made a mistake. I'm sorry. I'm just going crazy without you, baby. Think about poor little Maxwell and how he feels not having his daddy around him. You don't want to split up his family, do you?"

"He does need a daddy, but if you remember correctly, it was you who broke our family up by sleeping with Lucinda. I can't forgive you for what you've done and have Maxwell hurt again in the process. You even had the gumption to say you weren't even sure you were Maxwell's father. I have never been unfaithful to you. Never!"

"Tell me you don't love me, Cynthia, and I will leave and never show my face again."

"I don't know how I feel about you. I do know you are too drunk to get into a car. You might hurt someone, including yourself.

"Hold on there, Todd! You're not coming to our bed under any circumstances. You are sleeping on the couch! Hear me?"

"I hear you loud and clear, baby. You sure I can't sleep in bed with you after I take a shower?"

"Not with or without a shower. I'm done discussing it!"

Todd was not going to be sharing a bed with Cynthia tonight, but tomorrow night was a different story.

CHAPTER 31

THE NEXT MORNING, TODD WOKE up with achy bones from his night on the couch. *This will never do*, he thought to himself. He wasn't going to spend another night on the couch. Cynthia was angry with him, but he also knew she still loved him.

Maxwell would be waking up soon, and he needed to have some private time with Cynthia. He knew she had a hard time resisting him when they were in bed together.

He went upstairs and quietly opened the bedroom door. There Cynthia was, still asleep in their bed. Todd slowly slid under the covers until his hot, aggressive body was next to her. He gently began kissing her body until he could see her responding to every kiss and touch.

Todd was amazed with the power he had over women. To Todd, Cynthia was only a conquest. She was just one of many women he had worked his charms on. If his trusting little wife only knew Lucinda was not his only indiscretion in their marriage, she would have thrown him out a long time ago. What she didn't know wouldn't hurt her. For now, he knew he was back in the house, and she would forgive him sooner or later until he was caught again.

Things seemed to be going well for Todd until Cynthia realized what he was about to attempt in her half-asleep state, and she wasn't going to let that happen. How could Todd even attempt to climb into bed with her and do such a thing after breaking their marriage vows? Did he think she was an idiot who could pretend his affair with Lucinda never happened?

Cynthia pulled away from Todd and went immediately to the bathroom to get a shower. Before she closed the bathroom door, she turned around and said quietly to Todd, "We'll talk tonight!" Before Todd could say anything, Cynthia closed the bathroom door. He then heard the bathroom door lock.

He looked a little shocked, as he thought she had forgiven him and they were back together.

When Cynthia was finished in the shower, Todd took a quick shower and left for work. This was the first time he had ever seen Cynthia push him away. He did not expect this reaction from her and knew by the sound of her voice it would take some time, but sooner or later she would give in to his demands because he knew she loved him.

As Todd drove to work, he wondered if Lucinda would be begging him to take her back. He couldn't believe she had betrayed him. Was he not enough for her? She had really humiliated him by sleeping with that ignorant bookkeeper, Doug Mills. He would be doing his best to see that Mills got fired.

CHAPTER 32

WHEN TODD WALKED INTO HIS office at Jenson Pharmaceuticals, the place was practically empty except for the maintenance, cleaning crew that was just finishing up and Darlene Whitmore, Mr. Jenson's secretary.

Darlene was a thin, blond twenty-eight-year-old who had been with the company as a secretary for about five years. Just one look at her, and he didn't have to ask why they had picked her as secretary. It was hard to focus on her beautiful face because his eyes were always drawn to her low-cut tops that always revealed the cleavage of her breasts.

She was known to be flirtatious with the majority of male employees and male businessmen who came to the pharmaceutical company.

If there was anyone who could help Todd get rid of Mills, it would be Darlene. Todd was aware Darlene's son, Gabe, was the illegitimate son with her college boyfriend, Alex. Gabe, who was six years old, had some problems with his legs, and Darlene was accruing a lot of medical bills. He had a plan, and even though it would cost him money, he wanted to get rid of Mills. Todd walked over to Darlene to work his charm.

"So, Darlene, you're here really early today. How is Gabe doing?"

"Todd, you scared me half to death. I never expected anyone to be here this early."

"Just wanted to get started on some day's work is all. Of course, getting a head start on the day wasn't the only reason. I have been thinking a lot about you and Gabe. How is your son doing?"

"He seems to be doing better. The doctor seems to think it will probably only take another couple of surgeries to straighten them out. Of course, it will take quite a bit of physical therapy for him to walk again."

"I bet you have a lot of medical bills already."

"That's for sure, but I don't care as long as it helps him to be able to walk. There is no end to what a mother will do for her child, even without any help from the child's father."

"I'm really sorry you have to deal with all this by yourself, Darlene. It would mean a lot to me if I could help you out in some small way. I'm doing quite well here with my accounts, and it would make me feel good to help you out with some of those bills."

"Why would you offer to do that for me, Todd?"

"I feel bad for you being alone and having to deal with all this without the support of his father. First of all, I can't understand what father wouldn't want to be part of his son's life. There have been times in my life where it was hard to keep up with my bills. I always thought if I ever found someone in the same position and was financially stable, I would do what I could to help relieve their stress. It would really make me feel good if I could give you $15,000 to help you with his bills."

"You would do that for us, Todd?"

"Yes. We are friends, aren't we?"

"Yes, we are, Todd. I always knew you were a sweet man but never dreamt you were so caring."

"I have wanted to ask you if I could help but didn't want to offend you by offering."

"I think I could just cry. I have never had anyone be this kind to me. Your wife must be very proud of you."

"Now, don't go crying or you might get me crying, too!"

"Come over in about an hour, and I'll give you a check."

"Todd, you are the best! If there is anything at all I can do for you to repay you for your kindness, please let me know."

"There I go tearing up. They are happy tears for being able to help you. I only wish there was someone who could help me stop Doug Mills from seducing my wife and trying to get me fired in the process. My family means everything to me, and I don't want anyone trying to tear my son's family apart. I'm sure you can understand how hard it would be only having one parent raise you."

"Oh how awful for you, Todd. I can't believe he would be so cruel to do that to you, especially when he works in the same company as you. Is there anything I can do to help?"

"Not unless you have a way of getting him fired so he would have to find a job elsewhere, maybe out of state."

"No problem there. I can tell Mr. Jenson that Doug is making sexual remarks toward me and it makes me feel uncomfortable. Mr. Jenson is very much against things like that going on in the workplace. Doug does tell me how well I fit in my clothes and wiggles his eyebrows. I usually just ignore him, but because of what he is trying to do you and your wife, I will certainly tell Mr. Jenson how uncomfortable he makes me feel."

"You would do that for me?"

"Of course I would, Todd. You are a great asset to this company, and we can't have your job jeopardized. Mr. Jenson would be losing money if that happened."

"Darlene, I didn't give you the money so you would do a favor for me. I just wanted to help you."

"I know, Todd, but this is a small way that I can thank you for what you have graciously done for me. Please let me do this for you!"

"Thanks, Darlene. I have always said life is nothing if you can't help someone. Today is a good example of how we can show compassion for others."

Todd walked to his office, smiling all the way. Fifteen thousand dollars was a lot of money, but it was worth every penny to get Mills, the lowlife bookkeeper, fired for sleeping with his mistress. He couldn't wait to see Mill's face when he was being walked out of the building by security. This would teach Lucinda a lesson about cheating on him.

CHAPTER 33

TODD SAT AT HIS DESK waiting for Mills to be called into Mr. Jenson's office. When he saw the light on Mills's phone blinking, he knew it would be just a matter of minutes before security would be called to escort the bookkeeper out of the building.

Todd's concentration on what was about to happen with Mills was interrupted when he saw Lucinda walking toward him.

"Todd honey, I'm so sorry you walked in on Doug and me the other night, but we both had a little too much to drink. You know I love you, Todd. What happened with Doug was nothing."

"This is how you show me you love me? By sleeping with someone like Mills? I have treated you like a queen, Lucinda. If you want to slut around with him, you can, but he will have to be the one to buy you gifts and help with your bills. I don't think on his pay that is going to be possible, but it's your decision what kind of lifestyle you want to live."

"I told you it was only a fleeting moment of drunkenness. We, Doug and I, aren't a thing. You know you don't want to give me up. Cynthia can't make you feel like I can make you feel. Please forgive me, and it won't happen again!"

"I can this time, but you better never sleep with Mills or any other man again. If you do, it will be over for good between us. I can find numerous other female companions to satisfy my urges."

"Sorry, baby. I promise it won't ever happen again."

"It better not. You'll see what happens to those men you cheat with. I ruin them. They won't have two cents to rub together when I get through with them."

"I told you it won't happen again. What more can I do? Trust me! Come by my place tonight, and I will prove it to you."

"I'll come over after work, but I meant what I said about cheating on me."

Everything was going as planned. Suddenly, Lucinda and Todd heard a ruckus. Todd could see through the glass the expression on Mills's face. He could tell Mills was shocked. Just then, security walked into Jenson's office, escorting Mills over to his desk to gather his personal belongings. Mills was upset and verbally making it known to the office that he didn't deserve to be let go.

Lucinda watched and wondered why this was happening and was just about to say something to Todd when she looked over at him and noticed the expression on his face. She didn't have to ask him if he knew what was happening with Mills because the grin on Todd's face said it all. Todd said he would ruin Mills, and he had found a way. She now knew how vicious Todd could be toward people he wanted out of his way. She wondered if he would do the same to her.

CHAPTER 34

Cynthia was exhausted by the time she put Maxwell down for his nap. Her body was still sore from the accident, and it had been over a week.

Days in the Lives of Our Families was just starting, and she was anxious to see if Candace had awoken from her coma. She was wondering if Steven was the father of the baby that Candace was carrying.

Taylor was standing by her sister's bed crying.

"Candace, you've got to wake up. I'm so sorry I pushed you. I didn't mean to hurt you. I was so angry you wouldn't let go of Steven so we could be happy. I don't want you to die. If I thought there was any chance Steven still loved you, I would let him go. Please forgive me! You've got to be all right! I don't know how I will go on if something happens to you."

Taylor had been secretly seeing Steven for five months. He had told her he was not sleeping with Candace anymore. So how could Candace possibly be pregnant with Steven's baby? She wondered if her sister was having an affair.

All she wanted was for Candace to be all right and not to die. She would worry about what was to come of her relationship with Steven later.

As Taylor was still thinking about Steven, Taylor reached for her sister's hand and gently patted it. Candace opened her eyes and smiled up at her sister. Tears filled Taylor's eyes upon seeing Candace awake.

"I knew you would be here, Taylor," Candace said.

"You worried me so, Candace. I thought I had lost you," Taylor told her sister.

"Why am I in the hospital, Taylor? Where is Steven?"

"Don't you remember anything?"

"No, what is happening? Was I in a car accident?"

"Honey, I will answer your questions, but I need to tell the nurse you are awake. I'll be right back."

Taylor went to get a doctor. The doctor immediately came into the room with the nurse and examined Candace. Candace could not remember anything that had happened prior to her admission in the hospital. The last thing she remembered was her two-year anniversary, which was six months ago.

Candace had no memories of Steven and Taylor's affair, how she ended up in the hospital, or that she was two months' pregnant.

As Cynthia waited for the commercials to be over and *One Life to Give* to start, she thought about Todd. She was upset with him for coming back home and thinking she would just forget about his affair with Lucinda. He must have thought she was desperate and would just welcome him back home with open arms.

She was extremely hurt by his infidelity. Never in her wildest dreams had she ever thought he would be unfaithful to her. But he had been unfaithful! It would take a lot of time before she would ever get over what he had done to her, to their marriage, and to Maxwell.

Cynthia tried not to think about Todd because it was too painful. She was glad when her next story came on and she could get involved in someone else's twisted life.

One Life to Give began with Dr. Kindle taking over Dora's kidney transplant after Dr. Fred had a heart attack and died in the middle of the kidney transplant.

The surgery team worked for many tedious hours on the surgery. Dr. Kindle was very confident the surgery was a success. Their only concern now would be infection or rejection of the kidney. Dora's chances were about sixty-forty she would make a complete recovery, but it would be some time before they would know. It would be a long road for her, but she would have never had a chance without the transplant.

Cynthia watched these soaps and always felt good she didn't live such drama. She would never have thought her life would turn into a soap opera.

Any minute, little Maxwell would be waking up, and she looked forward to having time with the person who needed her the most.

CHAPTER 35

As Todd was leaving for Lucinda's, he noticed a message from his parents asking him to stop by their house on the way home.

He texted them back to let them know he would stop by for a few minutes before going home.

When he walked in the front door, he could see both his parents sitting in the kitchen.

"Mom, Dad … what's up?"

"Todd, your mother and I are quite upset with you. You have misled us and accused Michael in the process of having an affair with Cynthia. The truth is you are the one who is having an affair. The most precious thing a good man has is his family. A husband is supposed to cherish his wife and children."

"Dad, let me explain!"

"No, Todd! You do the listening while I am the one talking. We have always been proud of your accomplishments, but hearing you have dishonored Cynthia, your wife, by sleeping with your secretary has saddened us and lowered our expectations of you. There is no reason, no good reason, to have done this terrible thing to the mother of your child, not to mention you lied about your brother."

"Dad, you don't understand how Cynthia has changed since she's had Maxwell. We used to have fun together, and she always was interested in my job and us. Now, all she talks about is Maxwell this and Maxwell that to me. Lucinda has always been there to support me in all my accomplishments. She cares if I succeed. Cynthia doesn't care about all the hard work I do to give her a good life."

"I will repeat what I said one more time, so listen carefully, Todd! There is absolutely no reason you can give to make it all right to hurt your wife by sleeping with another woman. So you need to be a man by going home to Cynthia and apologizing for what you have done.

Promise her you will never commit this offense again and beg her to take you back, if not for her, then for Maxwell."

"I'm sorry I've disappointed you two, but it is my life, and I deserve to be happy. If Cynthia had been the woman I wanted, I wouldn't have had to find someone else to make me feel needed or meet my needs. So be disappointed, but I will do as I please with whom I please!"

Todd's father didn't say anything back to Todd as they saw him walk toward the front door and out of the house. Todd was fuming that his parents would tell him how to handle his marriage. He needed to be comforted, and the only person he thought would do that was Lucinda. She better be there for him like she said she would, or he would ruin her just like he ruined Doug Mills.

CHAPTER 36

TODD WAS SO HAPPY WHEN he finally got to Lucinda's. He couldn't believe his parents would even address him about his personal life. He wanted a woman who challenged him to do better and recognized him for all his achievements. Cynthia didn't care about him. She was too preoccupied with Maxwell.

Michael could have Cynthia. He could find many other women that wanted him and only him.

Lucinda had made a big mistake. She saw firsthand what would happen to anyone that tried to cross him. Hopefully she had learned a big lesson by seeing what he did with Mills.

Todd walked in the door to Lucinda's house. Dinner was not made like he had expected. Lucinda sat in a chair at the table, still in her work clothes. Normally she would be waiting for him in some enticing loungewear.

"Lucinda, what's going on? You knew I was coming over. Where's dinner, and why are you still dressed from work?"

"Todd … it's over with us. I saw what you did to Doug, and I don't want to be with you anymore. I don't trust you. I will admit I was wrong for sleeping with Doug. It was a mistake, and I admitted that to you. You said you would take me back, but taking me back came at a price for you getting Doug fired. How do I ever trust that you won't do that to me? All those times we slept together, I felt guilty because you were married. You promised me you would leave Cynthia, but I know you will never leave her. You never planned on it. It was just one great big lie to have us both. I should have never slept with a married man, especially since you have a son to think about."

"You're not going to do this to me, Lucinda. I have made life good for you, and without me, you won't last. I've already given you one chance, and I won't give you another. Do you hear me? I will let you rot before I take you back if you turn me down."

"I don't want another chance with you, Todd. What you did to Doug was terrible, and I can't justify being with you after getting him fired. You took his livelihood away from him. I will never forget that look on your face because it was so hateful."

"No one ever crosses me, not even you! So what is your decision? You better think long and hard before you answer."

"I am afraid of you now, Todd. I can't live like that."

"So maybe you shouldn't then! We're through, and I will destroy you like I did that idiot Mills."

"Todd, please don't do that to me!"

CHAPTER 37

CYNTHIA AND MAXWELL WERE SITTING on the floor playing when Todd walked in the door.

"Todd, what are you doing here?"

"It's my home, sweetheart."

"Todd, don't play games with me. You know what I mean!"

"Cynthia, you told me this morning we would talk tonight. That is why I'm here."

"When I said we would talk, I meant on the phone."

"Get over it, Cynthia! Lucinda and I are done. So I strayed. Big deal! Things happen in marriages that don't always make it perfect like you want it to be."

"Todd, I don't wish to discuss this in front of Maxwell."

"The kid is only two. He doesn't understand what we are even talking about."

"Maybe not, but I want him to live in a happy home."

"It is happy. Haven't I provided for you two good enough?"

"You are a great provider, Todd, but that doesn't make a happy home. You need to be there for us in more ways than financially. Maxwell needs his father to share in his life and someone to teach him how to grow up to be an honorable man. Frankly, I don't know if you are the one that can teach him because you have shown no respect for our marriage."

"Look! I told you I was done with Lucinda. I don't know how to be those things you want me to be. Can Michael be those things you're saying you want?"

"Don't go throwing Michael into this conversation. He has nothing to do with what has happened between us. It was what you did, Todd. I am deeply hurt by what you did. All those nights you told me you were working late were lies. Now you want to come back to the house like nothing is wrong. Everything is wrong, and the funny part of it is, you don't even realize you have done anything wrong."

"I told Lucinda it's over because I want to save my marriage. Do you want me to sleep on the street?"

"Why should I really care where you sleep after how you have hurt me? I am better than you are though. You can stay, but you're sleeping on the couch. Don't even attempt to try to sleep elsewhere! You can get yourself something to eat if you're hungry."

Cynthia turned and walked upstairs with Maxwell. Todd had never seen this side of Cynthia, but he liked it.

T HE NEXT MORNING, TODD WALKED into Jenson's Pharmaceuticals expecting to see Lucinda at her desk. Darlene Whitmore was sitting at her desk, so he walked over to see if she had heard anything from Lucinda.

"Good morning, Darlene."

"Good morning, Todd. I can't thank you enough for helping me with Gabe's medical bills. It feels really good to know I don't have all that debt over my head and can now provide us with other things we need."

"I am glad to have been able to help you, Darlene. You're a nice young woman who deserves a break. It is not easy when you don't have the support of Gabe's father. You work hard here and still are a great mother to your son. I try to be there for my son, and we don't have to deal with lots of medical bills for him. If there is anything else I can ever do for you, please ask. I consider you a good friend."

"Todd, you have already helped me. I appreciate your kindness. Gabe is everything to me. I didn't care about Alex not acknowledging Gabe being his son when he knew I was pregnant. Alex was in college, and I knew he didn't have extra money, but he has an education and is making good money now. It angers me that he doesn't care about us. Now with all the out-of-pocket expenses for him insurance doesn't pay, it would make it easier if Alex was helping. Thanks to you, his medical bills are paid off, and I have enough for his physical therapy. I owe you a lot, Todd."

"No thanks is necessary, Darlene. You just take care of that son of yours."

"I will, Todd. I better go see Mr. Jenson."

"Before you go see Mr. Jenson, can you tell me if Lucinda called off this morning?"

"Let me check my messages. I know she was crying yesterday after Doug got let go. I was really surprised because I didn't even know there was anything between the two of them. I felt bad for her, but from what you told me, he isn't the type of person we want working here. I do have one message from Lucinda. Let me check here … Lucinda said she is sorry but she needs to leave town. Something came up suddenly, and she doesn't know if she will be coming back. She said she enjoyed working here."

"Well, I guess I will be looking for a new secretary."

"That's too bad. She seemed to really like working with you."

"Yes, we did have a rapport."

Todd smiled at Darlene as she walked into Jenson's office. Lucinda was gone from his life. It had been good while it lasted, except for her indiscretion with Mills. Darlene was so easy. He knew he had her exactly where he wanted her, in the palm of his hand.

CHAPTER 39

MICHAEL COULD NOT GET HIS conversation with his parents out of his mind. He couldn't believe they actually believed Todd's fabricated story of Cynthia and him having an affair.

Even as they were growing up, their parents always seemed to think Todd was perfect. He wasn't perfect; he was just a great manipulator. Todd's success in being the top salesman in Jenson's Pharmaceuticals probably was due to his ability to manipulate people.

Michael could handle his parents thinking badly about him, but he couldn't take them thinking badly of Cynthia. He thought she was wonderful and was glad she finally knew how he felt about her.

He was glad she was through with Todd. He knew Cynthia was hurt that Todd wasn't the man she thought he was, but she would no longer have to put up with his excuses and infidelity.

Michael wanted to give her some time to deal with what Todd had done, but he longed to be with her and Maxwell as a family. He would do everything in his power to make them happy. Maybe someday they would even have some babies together. He wanted to be with them more than anything.

By now he figured his parents had called Todd to confront him with his lies. He wished he could have been there to see him squirm, but he probably would have punched him out for all his lies.

Just thinking about his brother made him angry, but those thoughts were soon overcome by good thoughts of Cynthia and Maxwell.

CHAPTER 40

MAXWELL AND CYNTHIA HAD JUST finished their breakfast and were waiting for Annie to come over with Annabelle and Andy for a playdate.

Maxwell was so excited; he kept walking over to the front door, watching for his cousins.

When they finally came, he gave his cousins a big hug and took them by the hand to his playroom.

"Do you want something to drink, Annie?"

"Coffee would be nice if you have some made."

"Sure do. I just put a fresh pot on. I have a coffee cake, too. Want a slice?"

"Of course I do. I can't say no to coffee cake. So … have you heard anything from Todd?"

"Yes, he said he broke up with Lucinda. He wants to come back home."

"You didn't say yes, did you?"

"Yes, but I told him he was sleeping on the couch and not to even attempt to come into the bedroom."

"Cynthia honey, you are too forgiving. I would have let him sleep on the street before I let him come back home after what he did."

"Regardless of how hurt I am by Todd, he is Maxwell's father. I owe it to Maxwell to give him a relationship with his daddy. None of this is Maxwell's fault."

"Sister, you are too, too nice. I do understand about none of this being Maxwell's fault or yours, for that matter. You're not remembering how Todd hasn't had much of a relationship with his son."

"I know, Annie, but if I don't leave those channels open, he never will be."

"Michael is crazy about Maxwell and you. Look how he stayed here and took care of both of you while that cheater husband of yours—"

"I know what Todd has done, but we are still married, and I can't look beyond that right now. I need to try to forgive him so we can try to save our marriage for Maxwell's sake."

"I don't mean to upset you, but I think Todd is interested in more than a place to sleep, especially since Lucinda and he are no longer together."

"I know Todd well, or I should say I thought I knew him well, but I can tell you he positively is not going to get from me what he wants. I can assure you."

"Well, if you ever are about to weaken and fall into his web, will you please call me first?"

"I am stronger than everyone thinks, but I'll keep you in mind for backup. So let's talk about something a little more exciting than my love life with my cheating husband or his brother."

"So … I have something exciting to tell you."

"Is it something more exciting than my drama?"

"I don't know if it could be more exciting … well, maybe it is."

"So what is it?"

"I think I'm pregnant."

"No crap!"

"No. I think it's a baby!"

"Of course it's a baby. I know you're not pregnant with crap. How far along do you think you are?"

"I am figuring six weeks, but I didn't want to say anything until I was pretty sure. At least the home pregnancy test says I am."

"Is Charlie happy you two are having another baby?"

"He is really excited. In fact, he was hoping we would having twins again. He said the more babies, the better. Can you believe that? I told him if that's the case, he can carry them this time."

"Let me know how that turns out. I talked to Marie last night. I told her you were coming over with the twins, and she might come over."

"I hope she does. Do you think I ought to tell her about being pregnant?"

"Marie will be happy for you. It's not like you can keep hiding the fact from her. We've all seen how you eat when you're pregnant. It's kind of a dead giveaway when you're eating for more than one."

"I did have a pretty hefty appetite when I was pregnant with the twins, didn't I?"

"Here's Marie now."

"Hello, sisters! How are you two doing? Where are those sweet little babies?"

"The three of them took off to play the minute we walked in the door. You seem to be in a very jolly mood today!"

"I am in a particularly good mood. I guess being pregnant does that to you."

"Oh my goodness! I am so happy it finally happened for you and Victor. Victor must be so excited. This is more exciting than me being pregnant again," Annie exclaimed.

"You have to be kidding, Annie. You're pregnant again?"

"I'm about six weeks. How far along do you think you are, Marie?" asked Cynthia.

"I'm about seven weeks. It looks like Annie and I will be having babies around the same time. Wouldn't it be funny if we delivered on the same day? What about you, Cynthia? You aren't pregnant too, are you?" asked Marie.

"No, that would be too much excitement for our parents to absorb. I am so excited for both of you, but I am totally out of the picture on this family project. Right now, that would not even be a remote possibility."

"That's not entirely true, Marie. Sweet Cynthia let Todd come back home. He's sleeping on the couch, but you know how that goes," said Annie.

"He broke up with Lucinda, Marie. I can't just let him sleep on the street. Can I? He is sleeping on the couch, not with me. After his escapades with Lucinda, I'm not going to forgive him for a long time. He has to prove to me he is going to be faithful and not ever do that again."

"Are you sure it's possible for Todd to be faithful, Cynthia?" Marie asked.

"I want more than anything for my marriage to work. You both should understand that. I don't want Maxwell to have divorced parents, but I do want him to be in a happy home. If for some reason Todd can't respect me and honor our vows, then I will have no choice but to leave him. He also needs to be a better father to Maxwell. In all of this … Maxwell is my main concern, and I owe it to him."

"Cynthia sweetie, I am on top of the world right now with finally getting pregnant. I thought Victor and I would never have a child. Annie and I both want you to be happy, too. Just because you love Todd doesn't mean he is going to make you happy. We do understand why you are trying to save your marriage, and we both would be doing the same thing if we were in your shoes. We will be with you no matter what you decide because we both love you," said Marie.

"I ditto everything Marie said, Cynthia. Now … let's get to celebrating and have a big piece of coffee cake, maybe two, because I am eating for more than one," said Annie as she laughed.

"Yes, we know very well how you eat when you're pregnant with two. If you were carrying more than two, there wouldn't be anything left for the rest of us to eat," laughed Marie.

"Ha … ha … ha. You two are so funny! By the way, what's for lunch?" Annie said as she giggled at the two.

"Yes, you sure are pregnant. Aren't you? I made chicken salad croissants," laughed Cynthia.

"That sounds yummy, Cynthia. Bring the food on!" Annie exclaimed.

"Do you think your poor little stomach can wait until we feed the three little ones and put them down for a nap?" asked Cynthia.

"I guess I could hold out. Maybe I'll just have another small piece of coffee cake until then," Annie replied.

"You have an appetite, sister. I hope I don't start eating like that with this baby. Right now, I am just having a lot of morning sickness. I'll put up with it to have our baby. Victor and I must have cried for two hours straight when we found out it was true because we were so happy," Marie told her sisters.

"It is a wonderful time in a marriage. Both Annie and I can testify to that. In most cases, it makes your marriage stronger," Cynthia said with tears in her eyes. She hoped her sisters couldn't see her tears because she didn't want to spoil their happiness.

"I'm sorry, Cynthia. Marie and I are both on top of the world right now, and you have to deal with Todd."

"Don't worry about me. I'll be all right. Let's just have a good time visiting, get the wee ones taken care of, and watch our soaps. Now there is some real drama!"

CHAPTER 41

MICHAEL HAD NOT SEEN CYNTHIA and Maxwell since he took care of them after the accident. He missed both of them so much.

His parents had told him they had confronted Todd about his affair with Lucinda. He informed Michael that Todd had broken it off with Lucinda and was living back in the house. He knew his brother's reputation with women and doubted if he could remain faithful to Cynthia. This would only bring her more heartache, and he didn't want her to have to go through it again.

It wouldn't be long before Todd found someone else to take Lucinda's place because he could never by happy with just one woman. He was a player, and his happiness depended on what he wanted.

Todd never wanted children. He didn't tell Cynthia that because she wanted to have a family. If she had known the truth, she more than likely wouldn't have married Todd because family was important to her.

Todd enjoyed a challenge, and Cynthia had been a challenge to him. Once he got her to marry him, his challenge was over. He loved women making a fuss over him and treating him like he was a king. Todd had already hurt Cynthia once. He knew Cynthia still loved him and would take him back for Maxwell's sake. Before all of this was over, Todd would probably hurt Cynthia again.

Michael couldn't bear to see his brother hurt her again, but it was inevitable. If she would only see Todd for what he was, she would be through with him and Michael could have a chance to make her happy. Until then, he would wait for her to have to choose between the two of them.

Michael was sorry his parents had to see this side of Todd. They had put him on a pedestal for long enough though, and it was about time they found out what kind of man he had grown to be. He was a man who took everything he wanted and stepped on everything in his way to get it.

Ben and he were nothing like Todd. Someday everyone would recognize the real Todd and no longer look at him as the person he portrayed himself to be.

Right now, all Michael could think about was Cynthia's sweet lips and how they felt when he kissed her as he confessed to her that he had loved her for a long time. He wondered if there would ever be more between them.

As Michael lingered on the thoughts of Cynthia and how deeply he wanted to be with her, he felt the need to see her. Maxwell would be down soon for his nap, and it would give him the opportunity to talk with her.

CHAPTER 42

Andy, Annabelle, and Maxwell were done with their lunch and down for their naps just as *Days in the Lives of Our Families* was starting. The three sisters were on the edge of their seats as they ate chicken salad croissants, waiting for the advertisements to be over.

Candace had just woken up from a coma as a result of bumping her head after her sister, Taylor, pushed her. From what the doctors could tell, she seemed to have lost all memory from her second wedding anniversary six months ago until now.

The three were so engrossed in the soap opera they didn't hear Michael walk in the door.

"Did I make it in time? I can't believe I almost missed the pivotal point in this soap opera."

"Michael Marshall, how do you always sneak up on us like that? You scared us out of our wits. Now sit down and behave yourself," Cynthia said.

"Do we have any tissues for the occasion? You know how sensitive I am," Michael added.

"Michael, I'll make sure you get a towel to dry those tears of yours," Cynthia said. "You poor, sensitive boy!"

"Hey, you two … take it to the kitchen. Can't you see Annie and I are trying to watch this story?" Annie said.

Michael smiled at Marie as he took his hand and pretended to be locking his mouth with a key. His eyes then moved from Marie to Cynthia, where he lingered on her beautiful face.

Cynthia glanced over at him and saw his eyes intense on her. She smiled at him and wondered if he could tell she was thinking about him kissing her.

Marie could see out of the corner of her eye Cynthia and Michael glancing at each other. She knew the real story was not the soap opera they were watching but what was happening between Michael and her sister.

"Taylor, why am I here in the hospital? I don't understand. Why can't I remember?"

"It's going to be all right, Candace. The doctors are going to take good care of you. Right now you just need to get better. I want you to know how much I love you."

"I love you, too, Taylor."

"This is so sad. I think I'm going to bawl my eyes out." Michael sniffled.

"You are more drama than the soap opera," Annie remarked.

"I can't help it, ladies! I just hate showing my softer side." Michael pretended to pout.

"Control your sobbing! *One Life to Give* is starting now," Marie said. "We'll have to have Cynthia take you to another room to watch it."

"Call Dr. Kindle, *stat*! The patient's temperature is spiking," said a nurse.

"We need to make the family aware the patient has developed an infection and is fighting for her life."

When Dora's family heard the news of her infection, they started praying Dora would make it through this setback. It was a miracle Dina's kidney was a match. They needed another miracle. She had made it long enough to find a match, and she just couldn't die now.

Suddenly alarms were going off. Dora's heart rate was dropping more.

"Crash cart *stat*!" yelled the head nurse.

"Please don't die, Dora. You can't. Not now!" exclaimed Michael.

The three sisters just shook their heads at Michael's drama. The three of them loved having Michael watch the soaps with them because he was so hilarious. Annie and Marie knew he wasn't really there for the soaps but because he wanted to be near Cynthia. The way he looked at her made it evident.

"You ladies relax and watch the last few minutes of your soap. I can get my niece and nephews up while you continue to enjoy."

"Well aren't you a sweetie? That's really nice of you," said Annie.

"I don't mind. I rather enjoy taking care of them any chance I get. It just gives me experience for when I have a bunch of babies of my own," Michael replied.

"I guess we will be giving you more practice because Annie and I are both expecting," said Marie.

"Well, I guess this is congratulations to both of you. I'll bet Victor is really excited, Marie. I know you've wanted this for a long time," Michael said.

"Victor is so excited. He is waiting on me like I was ready to deliver. He even wants to go out and by paint to start decorating a room for the baby. Isn't he funny?"

"No, he's just overjoyed like a father should be, Marie. I am sure I will be the same way, just thinking the woman you love is having your baby. Nothing is more important than family. Congratulations, Marie, and please tell Victor congratulations for me."

"Thanks, Michael. I will tell him," replied Marie.

"Congratulations to you, Annie, and of course Charley. I'm happy for both of you. The way the two of you are moving along here with your family, I better get me a wife quick! Any chance of another set of twins?"

"That is what Charley is hoping for, but it's not his stomach that has a hard time fitting through a door," said Annie.

"Well, let me know if Charley needs any help widening the doors," chuckled Michael as the girls laughed.

"I'm sure when you have your own children, you will be one of the best fathers there has ever been," said Marie.

"I am sure any woman would be happy to have you as a husband and father of her children," said Annie as she looked over at Cynthia.

"I have to go get the children up before I start crying," laughed Michael.

"Did he say *start*?" Marie said to her sisters as Michael was walking up the stairs.

Michael came downstairs carrying all three children. They were all fussing over their uncle Michael. It wasn't long before Marie, Annie, and the twins left. Michael missed not having children and a woman to love.

"Michael, I need to tell you something. Todd broke up with Lucinda, and he wants to come back home."

Cynthia watched Michael's expression. She didn't want to hurt him, knowing how he felt about her, but she had to be honest with him.

"My parents told me you let him come back home."

"I let him come home, but he is sleeping on the couch. I just wanted to explain to you why he's here. He said he made a mistake and he wants me back."

"Be careful, Cynthia. I don't want you to get hurt again by him. You can't trust him. One woman will never be enough to satisfy him, no matter how special she is. He always has a way of getting what he wants. Todd is such a fool; he doesn't realize that has the best there is."

"Michael, you don't need to worry about me. I know you want to protect me from Todd, but I have to do this for Maxwell. Please tell me you understand, Michael."

"I do understand, Cynthia. That is why I love you, because you always see the good even when it comes to Todd. Be very, very careful. Promise me, Cynthia!"

As Michael said this, he placed his hand on her cheek. Oh, how much he longed to hold her and kiss her. He wanted to protect her from ever being hurt because he loved her so much.

"If you need me, you know how to get ahold of me. I better leave before Todd comes home and I ruin things for you."

"Thank you, Michael, for caring so much. The three of us really had a good time with you."

"So did I. Being with the three of you and little Maxwell really made my day. If you need me for anything, you know you can call me."

When Michael left, Cynthia thought about how much she wished she were with Michael, but she just had to give Todd another chance to be a good father to Maxwell. She just had to!

CHAPTER 43

CYNTHIA HAD A WONDERFUL DAY with her sisters and Michael. She was so happy Marie was finally pregnant and Annie was adding to her family. She was looking forward to having another baby someday, but she wasn't sure if she wanted Todd to be the father.

Feeling this way made her sad because she never thought she would want anyone else to be the father of her children other than Todd because she loved him so much. A lot had happened since she was the crazy love-struck girl over Todd.

She had to wonder how her parents and brother would react when they heard Todd had an affair with Lucinda.

Her brother would probably want to beat Todd to a pulp. Sam was always so protective of his sisters. She would have been in favor of it if she weren't worried her brother would get hurt in the process.

As Maxwell played nicely with his toys, Cynthia started making supper. She wondered if Todd would be coming home for supper or if he would just come home to sleep. It made her nervous that he was back home because she was afraid of him, and she never had been before.

CHAPTER 44

TODD CAME HOME AT 7:00 p.m. Cynthia had just gotten Maxwell fed and ready for bed. It only took one look, and Cynthia knew Todd had stopped for a few drinks before coming home.

"Cynthia, did you make me some supper tonight?"

"Todd, I have everything put away. If you want leftovers, you will have to warm them up. I am going upstairs to read Maxwell a story before he goes to sleep."

"Can't you get me some supper first?"

"Todd, I'm going upstairs with Maxwell."

"I've worked all day, and I want you to get my supper. This is my house, and I pay the bills."

"I am not going to argue with you in your condition in front of Maxwell."

"As long as you are in my house, you will listen to me!"

"Todd, please lower your voice because you're scaring Maxwell. All I want to do is get Maxwell in bed."

"Do it then so you can get my supper!"

"Why don't you go get a nice shower, and then I'll sit with you while you eat dinner? It probably will relax you a little. You seem to be so stressed."

"That's more like it. It's about time you showed me some respect. A shower sounds good, and just to let you know, I'm not sleeping on the couch tonight or any other night."

Todd went upstairs to take a shower as Cynthia was putting Maxwell to bed. He was glad he put Cynthia in her place. He liked a little fire in her, but she was forgetting who was in charge. He felt tonight was going to be just like old times. Maybe Lucinda was not in the picture anymore, but tonight there was Cynthia. She would be useful for a while, but he could never be happy with just her.

He put on his sweats and went down to the kitchen to wait for Cynthia to finish with Maxwell. He waited another fifteen minutes for her to come down. He wanted his supper.

"What's taking her so long with that kid?"

He walked up the flight of stairs and opened the bedroom door. Cynthia and Maxwell were nowhere in sight.

What will happen next? Find out in book two, *Teardrops and Heartache.*

Future titles by Carla Kulka

Life Is a Soap Opera
Teardrops and Heartaches
Who's Crying a River Now?
Pass the Tissues Please!

Printed in the United States
By Bookmasters